STREETS OF NEW YORK

VOLUME

III

FOREWORD BY
TREASURE
BLUE

WRITTEN BY
ERICK S
GRAY

WRITTEN BY
ANTHONY
WHYTE

WRITTEN BY
MARK
ANTHONY

ISBN: 978-0-9792816-9-3

Novel by Anthony Whyte, Erick S Gray and Mark Anthony
Foreword by K'wan
Edited by Joy Leftow
Creative Direction & Design by Jason Claiborne

Augustus Publishing paperback May 2009
www.augustuspublishing.com

"Do not follow where the path may lead. Go instead where there is no path and leave a trail." – Ralph Waldo Emerson

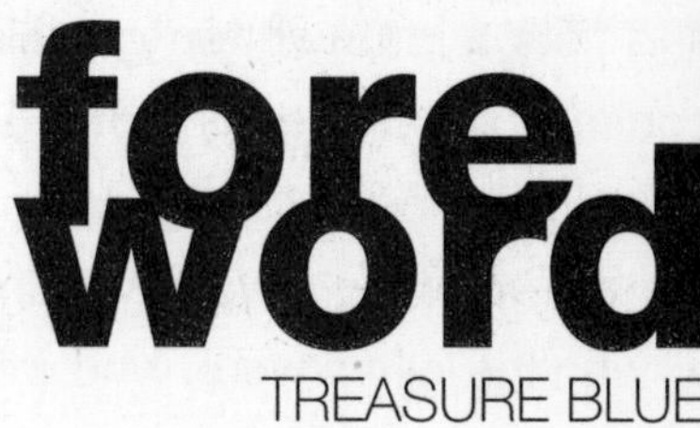

fore word

TREASURE BLUE

They say there are eight million stories in the naked city and if that's true the city of New York are the author of all of them. From Harlem to Queens, to Brooklyn to the Bronx, and even Staten Island, the streets are paved with unforgiving tales of disdain, destitution, and hopelessness because the city takes no prisoners. The streets of New York have spawned some of the most notorious underworld criminals in the history of America – Al Capone, Nicky Barnes, John Gotti and Frank Lucas, only to name a few, that ran the streets of New York by hook or crook. If there was a dollar to be made best believe it was going to be made – extortion, prostitution, drugs, thief and murder – bottom line was that a nigga was gonna eat by whatever method availed them. Even today, though the names have changed on the streets the game would never ever stop, it will always remain the same.

Growing up in Harlem in the early seventies was sort of paradise, a Mecca for a young black boy like myself to be attracted to this new found world that I never knew existed and it was there where I would earn my first degree - a P.H.D in common sense. Learning all the ghetto politics of juvenile delinquency such as playing hooky from school, short cons, gambling and petty theft's, I was behooved by the thrill of it all and took to it like a fish takes to water. You learn intuitively how to survive in the ghetto by wits and fists and unwritten guidelines. You learned if you wanted to continue breathing. One of the earliest rules I learned was to hear no evil, see no evil, and damn sure never speak no evil because the streets were always watching! It was common knowledge to all who the killers were, who was connected, who was the pushers and what spots were off limits to stick-up. Though murder was, and still is, a way of life on the streets, you know if a person got murdered, ten times out of ten he deserved it - your hood was the safest place in the world. Back in the day, old people, mothers and children could walk down the street without fear of being robbed or touched only because everybody looked out for each other. Even if by some small chance someone did violate the rule, like the man who once robbed an old lady for her Social Security check from a neighborhood check-cashing place. It would be years later that before something like that would happen again, because the violator would always be caught, thrown in a trunk, beaten over a course of two days, a inch away from death, then tied to the very gate of the check cashing place where he had robbed the old lady of her money. He'd be left nude, with a bloody note pinned through his flesh that read, 'I will not rob old ladies ever again.' written one hundred times. Street justice – city of New York

But even in such horrid conditions, the beauty of the street of New York has spawned some of the most famous, talented and gifted people the world had to offer. Sports stars such as Michael Jordan and Lew Alcindor, AKA Kareem Abdul Jabbar, noted spiritual and political leaders such as the Honorable Louis Farrakhan and Collin Powell and of course rap legends Biggie Smalls and Tupac Shakur. The list can go on and on. It was a haven for artistic talents to hone their craft and unfurl for the whole world to see. The streets of New York is a Mosaic melting pot where each generation learns from the latter and tests your heart to find out what kind of person you really are and leaves you with two simple choices: either persevere and stake your claim or fail and bounce back to where you came from by whatever boat, bus or train you rode in on.

Grand Master Flash and the Furious Five said it all when they rapped about the streets of New York

> "*New York, New York, big city of dreams and everything in New York ain't always what it seems, you might get fooled if you come from out of town, but I'm down by law and I know my way around!*"

I, for sure knows my way around. And I know one thing; if you can make it on the streets of New York, you can make it anywhere - that's my word!

STREETS OF NEW YORK
VOLUME III

a gangsta luv

ANTHONY WHYTE

Lindsay Roberts stared off into space. Her hazel eyes darted back and forth while her mind drifted on an empty log of premonitions. What if she hadn't let Squeeze take control of her life? Why hadn't she listened to her best friend; her mother and the advice given? She told her about this feeling, the one that haunts, that can't be ignored. A decision on whether or not you should turn around or keep it moving had to be made. Lindsay felt she had to do it soon. She had been holding on to something that might never have been, an illusion that was built within. Lindsay eyeballed the professor then turned her head to the text book on her desk.

She felt the tears forming in her eyes, felt them rolling pass her mascara and down her cheeks. Saddened she heard when her tears hit the paper, one at a time. Lindsay slowly attempted to regain the feeling which she hoped would keep her head from swimming. She dried her eyes and attempted to refocus on the lesson at hand: Accounting 101. Professor Allen was in charge and he was nice gentle older man. This used to be her favorite class before today came along.

She'd skipped two other classes, spent time inside the cafeteria trying to hide tears of disgust. Lindsay decided to attend this class. It was her favorite class except after she had arrived she wasn't much in the mood to hear anyone speaking. Lindsay was caught in a cloud of anxiety. Life had not been what it was since Squeeze went missing in action.

He had broken his commitment to her. "A man be there for you until it no longer interest him", her mother had warned. It was with these anxieties that she had dared to enter her accounting class. Lindsay thought it would raise her spirits. And maybe some of what she felt when she first registered for the class could be recaptured. At least that was the rationale. Now Lindsay wished she had not set foot in the classroom especially with professor Allen teaching. She had opened up to him, they had formed a bond and he had always encouraged her. He probably felt he knew her. The professor had told her she was strong, proud and intelligent when she applied herself. Today, it wasn't in the cards, Lindsay thought as she looked at his face. He smiled, nodded and she felt his attitude already irked her. Oh, by the way, Professor Allen today I'm weak, feeble and didn't really feel like applying myself, Lindsay wanted to say. Instead she stared blankly at the chalkboard.

Round and round her wits swirled blurring her vision of reality. She paid very little or no attention to the words spoken by the talkative professor, or the balance sheet which he directed the class to research. Lindsay turned and eyeballed the classroom. It lacked warmth, the buzz of the hopefuls had simmered and it appeared smaller than when she started the semester. The hopeless had slowly dropped the course. Now was it her turn? Her mind whirled in sadness and Lindsay's heart pounded a heavy beat.

A cold spell caused her slim frame to shudder. She pulled her Hermes scarf closer to the olive skin of her long nape. Lindsay felt as if she was sitting on a chair of pine cones. Accounting was her last class of the day and so far that was the best thing about today. She had to survive another day, go another round with nothing but Squeeze left on her mind. It was fall, she reminded herself but in her mind it was the dead of winter.

The vibrations from her cell phone jolted her. Lindsay

glanced at the phone with heavy expectations. It wasn't Squeeze. He was stored in her phone's memory as H4L. Mother appeared on the screen. Lindsay quickly turned the phone off. Her actions caused the professor to take unwelcome notice of her.

"Ms. Roberts are you following along with us so far?" The professor asked.

Lindsay nodded and shirked her brow skyward and then looked away. She attempted to hide her feelings by staring at her text book. Lidsay used to open the book and glance at the pages with lots of pride. That was then. Now all that seemed to have been a passing phase. Attending college was no longer interesting.

The newness of learning had faded and could not impede her thoughts. Mother was probably calling her about going out to dinner or shopping. Lately, they seemed to be doing that an awful lot. Mother had always insisted on treating, Lindsay wondered where she had been getting all that money. She probably spent all that dough Show gave her, I know my mother; she's a survivor. Maybe she's just calling to see if I'm okay. I mean I did keep her up all last night on the phone.

I can't say she didn't warn me of days like this, Lindsay sighed. She was sure that things would be better if Squeeze just call her. Instead of trying to drag herself off the floor she would've felt great about being a college student and her spirits definitely would have been boosted. Lindsay knew she'd be more in the mood for rushing to meet deadlines, classes and writing papers, even communicating with her professors. But today was just not that type of day. On this fall afternoon in late September Lindsay regretted ever signing up for classes at York College.

In the beginning she liked the way Squeeze introduced her to associates and pals as his college girl. The aura completed her, made her feel respectable. It was mostly from the urging of Squeeze and her mother that kept her motivation level high enough for the college courses. But it was mostly Squeeze.

"Just take a few classes. See if you like it. I'm a be there for you no matter what, baby-doll," he had insisted.

It would've been a lie if she told anyone that Squeeze had not been supportive in every way possible. And he always wanted her to be better. He was lways encouraging her. In return she wanted him to feel good about her success. So she tried. Thrill went through her entire frame when he used to smile and utter the words: "That's my baby-doll."

Hearing it roll off his lips and the way he looked at her made Lindsay proud to be alive. She felt like she belonged to someone who loved her. Squeeze was hers and she was his even if it was only a fantasy she made up. Her logic; he was only thugging and didn't want to say the three words. Squeeze was committed to the streets and Lindsay knew that in the streets, you live whenever you can. Nothing ever went on a smooth schedule. Things get done when they got done.

Squeeze would see her when he could. That was her creed and Lindsay wanted to live by it. Except, Squeeze had turned her out and she loved the good life. Everyday with Squeeze brought a new and pleasant surprise. He spent quality moments with her which led Lindsay to think that things would remain the same forever. Squeeze let her ride and she earned her stripes. Lindsay knew it would be impossible for him to leave his family, home, and his two sons whom he constantly bragged about.

Still she had let Squeeze into her heart as a lover and friend, he was her backbone. Lindsay knew he loved her. She'd felt it from the beginning. Even back in the days when Squeeze only used to visit her brother, Pooh. He used to give her the type of looks that would say a lot more. Although she was only a shortie those passing glances between them spoke volumes to her.

"Baby-doll, Pooh, here?" She remembered him asking with that fly look of his and a wink. Squeeze always checked out her style and he'd compliment her too. "You lookin' really good an' you getting' taller, baby-doll. How old are you?" Squeeze would ask. She wouldn't say her age because she was afraid he'd say she was too young. So she always gave the same response.

"I'm old enough for whatever man."

"For whatever, huh?" Squeeze would ask and she thought she was getting closer to him but then Pooh popped up.

"Lindsay ma want you upstairs."

"Liar, I just came outside. Mommy knows."

"Just take your young ass upstairs." Pooh would say. He acted like he was my father. Lindsay remembered thinking.

"Oh let shortie hang out a few." Squeeze always stuck up for her.

She liked when he paid attention to her and his eyes always roamed, from head to heels. Lindsay knew Pooh didn't want her nowhere near the streets so she kept all those feelings under wraps. Now her brother was no longer here, she felt it was okay. Lindsay had Squeeze on her mind when she had gone to the Brooklyn club owned by Squeeze and his partner Show. Lindsay went with her then boyfriend, Malik. Show was there trying to be the man. He had let them inside and she was feeling him for a minute but had played him off when he tried to get ass. Show really pushed up hard on her.

Then a supernatural thing happened when she saw Squeeze. It was over. That night in the club, she laid eyes on him, her skin tingled and her throat went totally dry. Malik became invisible as the beam from her eyes was focussed on Squeeze. Lindsay remembered thinking I knew him when. And he'd come a long way from regular hustling and thugging to owner of the hottest weekend jump-off in BK. He was the epitomy of the powerful gangsta Pooh told her they all aspired to be. And Squeeze was even more handsome. Squeeze and Show had surpassed everyone's expectations. Lindsay felt the attraction returning even stronger. She remembered how regally gangster he looked as he walked to the table sat and said:

"Lindsay, Pooh's lil' sis? How're you doing?" His voice immediately put her in the mood for sex and they did the do.

Ever since they had hooked up, about three months ago, Squeeze had made a point about being there for her. Physically he broke her off but mentally she had him loving her even though she knew that he could never guarantee that emotion. It was like that because Lindsay wanted it like that. She told herself things would only get better and she faced the world wide-eyed thinking that Squeeze would be there just in case she fell. Lindsay would make him fall in love and maybe, just maybe he would leave his family for her. She thought about it and quickly realized that if it didn't happen that way she really didn't mind sharing him.

His wifey could have him as husband and father at home. But Lindsay knew Squeeze would come back to the streets and when he did, she'd be there for him. She'd be wifey to the hustler inside of him. Squeeze had told her once that he was a hustler for life and thus his moniker H4L. She knew as long as the hustler lived he'd always be by her side. Lindsay heard the professor but gently tuned him out as she gave way to her feelings and reflected.

In a short time, he had transformed her from a chicken-head stuck in a relationship that was going-nowhere into a blinging loudly frosty name brand wearing fashion plate. She had a boyfriend who worked for Footlocker, now Squeeze treated her to the finest of everything.

"I love to see you dressed up baby-doll. Always stay rocking the best gears, compliments of your main Squeeze." He had bought her so much clothing she showed up late to every event including classes because it took her forever to decide on what to wear.

Lindsay boasted Foxes, Chinchillas and couture that were the finest brands. Neighbors started hating when a rumor that she had expensive outfits for everyday of the year was leaked by her mother. Lindsay recalled sitting in the living room with her mother and relating an incident which occurred one evening as she walked home from the train station. Her mother had made light of the whole incident. Yet Lindsay was shook by what had happened.

"Mommy I swear, he followed me all the way home and then he tried to slow me down by asking what time it was?"

"He could've just seen how nice you looked and was trying out a pick–up line, honey. These young thugs out here, they respected your brother's way of life, they're not gonna disrespect Pooh's little sis."

"No mommy he was straight up trying to rob me. He asked me what time it was. Any man trying that line is trying to rob you."

"You can't be serious Lindsay? You thought it was a scam?"

"I mean the time, who cares about the time? I was hollering at him to back up before his ass gets hurt."

"Lindsay you can't go around challenging these young riff-raffs."

"Why not, mommy? They bleed just like I do."

"Yes, they do Lindsay. But any damn little thing and they ready to shoot you. And I cannot afford to lose you. You're all I have left in this world. You know your brother…"

"Yeah mommy you're right," Lindsay had said after sitting and thinking. "You know what I'll do?" Lindsay asked. Before her mother could reply Lindsay suddenly blurted out: "I'll ask Squeeze to help me find a better place." No sooner had the words left her lips than her mother began ranting and raving.

"Squeeze, Squeeze, Squeeze! That's all I ever hear you sayin'. Is that your new anthem? Wha' happened to ah…what's his name?"

"You mean Malik?"

"Yes that one. Him. What happened to him? "

"Nothing why? He's doing him. I'm about me."

"Be about you and not about no man, cuz let me tell you girl, a man will leave you hangin' at anytime it pleases him. You'll be stuck out there all alone."

"Mommy it ain't like that between me and Squeeze, he just like to look out cuz, we like, ah you know? Family. I mean he knew my brother, your son as well as we did. You even said Show," Lindsay paused and stared at her mother, "looked out for you. Mommy you know Squeeze, Show and Promise, they were Pooh's best friend. They're like our extended street family. They were my brother's best friends."

"Extended street family, huh? Tell me what's really up with you an' Squeeze? Why is he so interested in your welfare?"

"Ma, don't sweat it. It's not really like that."

"Humph! All I'm saying is don't grow to be dependent on no man. They're out to get sump'n too. He's always giving and you always taking, one day you may have to pay for it. And paying might not be what you want to do at that time."

Lindsay remembered her mother's words. Squeeze never asked for any payment in return and if he did Lindsay knew she'd gladly give it up. Lindsay was concerned about being made a victim by a hater from her Brooklyn hood, and asked Squeeze to get her an apartment.

Squeeze promptly did and moved her into her own furnished one bedroom dig, in a nice building with a view of the Bay in Queens. Squeeze helped Lindsay developed her driving skills. One month after passing her road test, she was presented with her own whip, a white convertible BMW 645i.

Lindsay took pride in knowing she had her own apartment, and now an official member of the BMW set. Who would have guessed that couple months ago she was riding in Malik's bucket with him pawing her, and she trying to figure what she wanted to do next. Lindsay had quickly become an adult with no plans, at nineteen years old. She was getting used to staying at home with mom.

Then along came Squeeze and her self esteem vaulted to new heights. Especially when he started to shower her with diamonds and pearls. At first she thought he was kind to her because she was Pooh's little sister, after all her dearly departed older brother had been best friends with Squeeze.

Things became sad when the potholes of street living snapped her brother's life short. Life seemed dim then she met and fell in love with Squeeze. To Lindsay it was like having a big brother, lover and friend, all rolled in one. Squeeze never tried to replace Pooh but he was happy he had Pooh's sister.

"I guess hazel eyes run in y'all fam. For real, you wear it the best, baby-doll," he smiled and said on that magical night.

The unexpected happened in a flash; the killing of Show and the shootings at the club owned by Squeeze and Show. As if that wasn't enough, all of a sudden she couldn't get at Squeeze. Her constant worrying drove her straight over the precipice of hopelessness and into a funk that threatened to end at insanity. Lindsay hadn't heard from him in such a long time she became convinced that the ride on easy street was absolutely over.

Lindsay was certain that the relationship between her and Squeeze meant something. She knew that despite having a family out in Carnesie he would spend a lot of time with her doing fun things. Squeeze used to take her out to parties on phat yachts and they would spend nights on the town having expensive dinners in new restaurants. She went to hot places that she had only dreamt of and either seen in the movies or on television.

Squeeze flat out spoiled her and he broke her off with exquisite sex. Blew my back out, Lindsay recalled and unconsciously she rubbed her swollen breast. She missed

Squeeze so much that her mesh stockings gripped her tighter and she could feel the wet spot growing wider. Lindsay's thighs involuntarily shuddered as if she was caught in a winter's storm. We used to see so much of each other.

Her ruminations were perplexing enough without her trying desperately to remember the last time she had felt Squeeze's full lips on her body. Oh, how he used to make me feel so good, Lindsay's thought continued to stray. It had been over a month now and even though all the bills were taken care of, she could still feel her body slowly awaking from the thoughts of losing him.

Sitting in the second floor classroom Lindsay's musings came like a drunkard staggering back and forth. Squeeze was heavy on her mind and her concern grew so strong that she could not focus on any other single thing and gave up trying all together. What's the use she couldn't front, school was for the birds, Lindsay told herself. Now exhausted from stressing she sighed and gave into her longing.

It bothered her that she'd left a couple dozen messages on the voice mail to his cellphone. There had been no return calls. The sound of his voice was no longer there to provide the encouragement she needed to stay strong. There were no responses from him. Mentally she wasn't ready to tackle the issue of whether or not something was wrong with him.

Maybe his family found out about her and he had to lay low. Or, maybe after the shooting outside his nightclub that left all those patrons on line dead, he had to disappear for a while. She was drowning in a sea of uncertainty, where high waves dashed all her hopes against rocks. She was twisted on a love that never was.

Lindsay felt all her energy being sapped by the bad vibe she received. Then a thought appeared in her head. She contemplated driving to his home. Squeeze had forbid her to do so. She didn't want to violate his policy but Lindsay desperately wanted to hold on to her sanity.

Thinking like this made it difficult for her to concentrate or participate in the various sides of the ledger activities. Accounting 101 used to be her favorite class, because it dealt with money. Lindsay liked money. No, Lindsay loved money. She kept telling herself that she didn't want to aspire to gold-digger status. Lindsay enrolled in some classes at York College. She was the first one to do so from her family. Her mother never made it past Junior High and her brother quit school in the 7th grade.

Lindsay had planned to complete her studies and move on to a four year college. She wanted to eventually run her own accounting firm. Today she hated to sit in the class and couldn't wait for the time to go by. Not wanting the professor to see her, because she knew how much he hated students who did it, Lindsay glanced at her Gucci timepiece with quickness, but the professor was aware of her moves.

"Your bling will only carry you so far but with knowledge you will go all the way. Ms. Roberts, please explain what goes on the left side of the ledger and what goes on the right and the reason for your answer." Lindsay held his stare for a minute and then cursed under her breath. "Yes, I'm addressing you Miss," the professor assured Lindsay, her expression was more like a deer caught in a headlight than an attentive college student.

"This geezer is irking the fuck outta me." Lindsay muttered under her breath.

"I'll speak with you after class. If you want, right now you're holding up the rest of those who actually care if they learn something."

"You the one addressing me, it ain't like I said anything to disturb your class. And I most certainly don't wanna speak to your ol' ass. Humph, humph uh-uh don't lemme act da fool up in here, ahight. Just keep on teaching and leave me the hell alone."

"Lindsay you're a good student but that attitude will only cause you problems. I will not stand for your insolence! I'll continue this discussion with you later young lady."

"No, you won't."

"Yes I will. Now let's move on..." the professor walked away.

"No you will not." Lindsay muttered under her breath.

Lindsay sighed and spent the rest of the time nervously doodling as the professor rambled on. Nothing seems to matter today. Really, Lindsay could care less about the debit and the credit side of the balance sheet. She knew the professor was right. I should be paying attention she admonished herself. This is for me, for my brother Pooh, my mother. This is to prove that one of us could do sump'n right. But I worry so much about other things this classroom thing is difficult. My mind is stuck on one thing and it ain't this, Lindsay reasoned.

As much as she tried she couldn't get out of her mind all the things had happened. Malik had been shot to death. Although Squeeze claimed that he didn't know anything about it, she was having major difficulties believing him. When she had pressed him he got mad and screamed at her.

Squeeze had called her a nag and things were out of hand.

She had said some things she shouldn't, called him names. Now he was staying away and she missed him. The club had been shot up and patrons were staying away so the place had been closed up. Lindsay had no way of contacting Squeeze except to visit him at home. That was out of the question, she thought.

"Everything is balanced when debit and credit are equal. A profit is gained as your credit becomes lower..." the professor was heard saying.

Lindsay could care less, the equation she worried most about was the one going down between her and Squeeze. She loved him and even though he had not actually said it, she believed he felt the same way about her. She missed him and wished he would stop in and see her. Maybe he would meet her in the parking lot like he used to. She was wishing so hard she paid no mind to the professor and his sarcastic goodbye.

"Those who are able to concentrate in class may read ahead and do the examples on pages twenty-three to twenty-six. That's only for the students who would like an A or A plus. Or those who would like to someday graduate and move on."

Lindsay disregarded the professor's final remarks and hurried from her accounting classroom. She sensed that he'd only said that last piece because she'd share this with him. She hated him for exposing her, putting her feelings on full blast.

"Lindsay, Lindsay what's the rush I know for a fact that you've got no other classes at this time. Would you like to talk?"

She stared at the professor, despite their run-in earlier he was trying to smile. Lindsay had no time for his tired ol' ass. Lindsay thought of an escape plan with the quickness.

"Professor, I gotta go, okay."

"C'mon, you said you would talk to me if anything went wrong. I'm a friend remember. Why it seems like just last week we were talking, and you said I was your favorite professor. Those were your own words," he said getting closer.

She was searching for a qick exit. The professor was persistent and getting closer.

"I... I," she started. He waved, quickly cutting her off.

"C'mon, c'mon, Lindsay let's have two small cups of coffee and a big chat. You did say we would always discuss things. C'mon tell me what's wrong, you're my best student. You've always aced my class and when I see you falling off well, I just gotta let you know. In order to assist you, I gotta know what's going on."

"Professor Allen, I'll speak with you next week. Right now I really gotta go!" Lindsay exclaimed.

Suddenly she turned hiding her tears. The professor tried to catch up to her but Lindsay was off and running for the stairs. She could hear the professor calling her name out as she continued on her way.

"Lindsay, Lindsay?" The professor stood and stared as the young girl disappeared down the spiraling staircase. He shook his head and walked away. "These kids are under too much stress. No time for anything. No time."

Lindsay moved swiftly out of range. She knew he wouldn't shout, he didn't believe in shouting and she didn't feel like talking with him. I can't believe I used to think he was my favorite professor, she thought as Prada heels clicked loudly through the halls and quickly across the busy street. It was a little after two in the afternoon as the eight cylinder of the silver BMW 645ci, roared. Lindsay, her remote in hand, hurriedly approached it. Her short denim skirt was stretched to the limit as she entered the car. Lindsay peeled off with attitude and desire. Now I've got to drop that course, she thought while staring at traffic.

Picking up her cellphone, scanning for her messages, Lindsay dialed frantically as the white convertible dodged traffic. Her thoughts raced, wondering about her lover. Squeeze hasn't even called me back already. It's been a fucking minute now. Lindsay's thoughts raced as she hit the brake for a stoplight. She paused, refreshed her lip gloss then dialed quickly. Again all she got was his outgoing message.

"Squeeze," she yelled into the cell phone. "Squeeze, I miss you so much Squeeze. Hit me back boo. Call as soon as you get the chance, honey." She felt pitiful, sorry for herself but she needed him to spark her. Lindsay wished he'd pick-up his phone when she called, wished he was there with her when she needed him.

If wishes were horses, I'd have a stable fucking with you Squeeze. Lindsay set the phone down and continued to drive. She pressed the remote to the radio when she got tired of listening to her own thoughts. The Game and 50 Cent thumped *How We Do*. Lindsay pumped up the volume and hummed along.

"*This is how we do… we making move act da fool while
we up in da club
This how we do… nobody do it like we do so
show us some love…*"

No matter how hard she tried, the voices she heard in her head could not be ignored, mainly the one that instructed her to drive to Squeeze's home. She had a full tank of gas and was ready to ride. There was no one else here to check her actions. Lindsay would have no one but herself to blame if anything went wrong. She realized this action would be entirely on her. Then she told herself it was now or never.

Mentally Lindsay rationalized: She just wanted to take a look and see if he was all right. Just drive around to his neighborhood maybe peek and make sure he was still breathing. I owe him that much, Lindsay thought as she struggled with the stress of her dilemma. The music reverberated from speakers as Lindsay tried to deal with the voices she heard in her head. 'Wait a minute' the sound of Ray J with Lil' Kim came through her speakers.

...It's on tonight... Wait a minute , wait a minute...

Throwing caution to the wind, Lindsay did not heed the chorus as she steered the car farther from home.

"I'll deal with the consequences later," she told herself as the BMW darted to the Expressway. She thumbed the steering wheel and sung to her favorite tunes on the radio. Many songs later Lindsay found herself closer to her destination. Lindsay let the car roll down the block made up of rows of well kept trees on either side, which provided shades for expensive mansions. She peered hard when she thought she saw his Escalade sitting in the driveway.

Lindsay was certain this was the right one, she could identify his personal tags HFL1, an acronym for hustler for life one. It crossed her mind to go right up to the front door and ring the bell, but she quickly dismissed the thought. Squeeze would be too through with her, she did not dare risk his anger. She wasn't here to cause any beef, or stir up problems with his family. She just wanted to make sure he was alright. But exactly how was that going down without her really asking someone inside?

Lindsay sat in the car and contemplated the possibility of ringing the doorbell and running, she could hide near the well trimmed bushes. Then as if in answer to her wishes the door opened and she could see Squeeze, but he was with someone else maybe that was his wifey. Thinking and acting real fast Lindsay got out the car and ran over to Squeeze.

"'Scuse me, 'scuse me, I'm sorry but I'm lost. Could you like...ah show me where the highway is, mister?" Lindsay asked with an air of sarcasm. Squeeze did a double-take and almost blew it.

"Lind..." Squeeze paused and stared at the driver in amazement. "Yeah, I could show ya, ma." He spoke and walked quickly to where she stood. "Just go a few blocks and make a sharp right," Squeeze said in a loud voice. He watched her raise her eyebrow and under his breath Squeeze quickly hissed at her. "What da fuck you doing round here, bitch?"

Squeeze was up close and personal now. Lindsay could smell the Issy Miyake cologne she'd bought him. He looked good and he was alive. She wanted to reach up caress his face and kiss his moist lips. There was no denying his anger. "How many times I done said it bitch? You stupid or sump'n, huh? You lost your fucking mind? I thought I told you not to come to my muthafucking rest. I'll get in touch with you later. Me and the wifey making some moves right now, I'll come check you later, ahight?"

"Okay, I hear you. I hear you. It's so good to see you, Squeeze honey. I didn't mean to put the BI on Front Street. I'm sorry boo."

"Don't worry bout a thing, ma just make sure you don't

make the wrong turn again, that's all. Go straight take that left and be on your way. Drive safely. And be home, ahight. I'll see you later."

"For real, for real Squeeze? Say you promise, please."

"Wha' I say, just be at your fucking place an' be ready. I'm coming to break you off sump'n, baby-doll."

"I could use the stress relief. Feel me Squeeze?" Lindsay reached up to touch Squeeze's face but he grabbed her arm a little too rough. Disappointed that she couldn't receive more attention, Lindsay headed to her car. "I'm sorry it was tempting that's all," she said as she got back in the car.

"I'll see you later, baby-doll."

"It's so good to feel you Squeeze." Lindsay peeled off.

Squeeze turned and walked slowly back to the front door. He knew that wifey had probably peeped the happening and was waiting to set it on him. Lindsay had compromised his home life. He had been meaning to have that talk with her about blowing up his cell phone. Squeeze realized he definitely needed to have that talk with her real soon.

Bitch be thinking it'll be the same ways e'erday. Lindsay is wilding out I gotta go holla at her ass later, Squeeze thought as he approached his wife. From the way she was fixing her lips, he could tell it was on.

"Why was that bitch all up in your grill like that Squeeze?" His wife asked immediately.

"Whoa, what you talkin' bout? Ain't none o' that goin'on?"

"Ain't no bitch up in your face, either huh?" She asked slyly.

"Hold up. Wha' bitch you talkin' bout?" Squeeze was not about to say anything until he knew exactly what she'd seen.

"The bitch who just drove off. Don't play me for a sucker, Squeeze. The bitch..."

"Who da' honey back there? Oh, you talkin' bout someone who loss they way an' I'm trying to help out?" Squeeze asked feigning ignorance.

"Yes Squeeze, the one who was just now all up in your grill. That's the only one I seen. Are there more? She had all the extracurricular goin' on. What? You had to exchange phone numbers or sump'n?"

"Listen; don't start with that BS, man. Honey just thought I looked like the movie star, Omar Epps from Queens. And was giving me some props that's all," Squeeze shrugged.

"Oh, that's how you get down. That's how you be pulling them hootchies, you better watch yourself Squeeze. Them same hootchies and bitches might be your damn downfall. And when you're gone these kids and me will starve tryin' a survive."

"Don't start kicking dust on me, I ain't dead yet." Squeeze warned before adding. "Let's go get these groceries and feed my sons. I got some things to take care of later."

"It ain't got nothing to do with that girl mistaking you for Omar Epps do it?"

"C'mon, stop playing. You ready? Cuz I'm fittin' to go right now. You hear? You know how those places be crowded on a Friday evening, lines be long," Squeeze said and started the engine.

"Stop the whining...? Squeeze you know since the last couple months you been here eatin' like everyone else does round here."

Squeeze watched his wife climb cautiously into the wifey ride, his white Benz. No one else was allowed but wifey, she had made him swore.

"C'mon hurry. You moving like you pregnant," Squeeze said to her.

"Oh no, please don't say that. I just pushed out one more of your boys, my ovaries are not rested enough. Give it some time. I'm just tired. I've been the one taking care of your hard headed sons."

"I've been here helping."

"True, only for the past month or so, that's the most I've seen of you. The world must be coming to an end."

"When I'm not here, you got your mother. She's always helping you out."

"Ahight, ahight stop complaining. I'm in the car and my seatbelt buckled now go, Omar." She laughed and Squeeze had no choice but to smile.

"Funny, very funny, keep it up and see if you go to the mall."

"Okay, I promise not to call you Omar ever again. I promise Mr. Epps. Squeeze you gotta take me to the mall. You know how good it feels to walk around and smell…What?"

"See, you broke your promise already."

"How?"

"Cuz Epps is part of Omar."

"Alright, I promise not to call you anything other than baby, if you take me shopping at the mall. I'm free - no children to bother me."

Squeeze smiled and she continued. "I'll just call and tell mom that I'll be later so she won't worry." She attempted to use her phone but realized instantly that there was no charge on the battery. She turned to her husband and said: "Squeeze lemme borrow your phone real quick please." Before Squeeze could direct his wife as to which of his three cell phones to use, she arbitrarily picked the one with unanswered messages. "You better answer all your fan calls O. I'm sorry," she laughed.

"Here use this one, smart ass," Squeeze replied smirking and redirecting his focus to the road ahead.

FOR EVERY ACTION THERE'S A CONSEQUENCE

Lindsay heard her cellphone ringing as she drove home. She slowed her mind enough to answer. Wishing that Squeeze's number would appear on her caller ID made her so excited, her heart palpitated. His presence had left her with a giddy feeling, she was riding high. Reality check: Mother again. "Hey mommy, I gotta call you back I'm driving home."

"Lindsay have you been drinking? You sound like you drunk or you found Jesus. You best slow your role, girl."

"Mommy, you worry too much. I'm alright. I just wanna get home early to fix up the place a little."

"Why, are you expecting your main Squeeze to come by?"

"Mommy, gosh no. I didn't tell you? Some of the girls from my class are dropping by to discuss accounting problems. Everyone likes my place."

"Oh you're hosting a party for the students of your favorite class?"

"Sump'n like that."

"In that case have fun. I was gonna suggest we go out for a little mother and daughter dinner but since you're busy and all. I mean you've been moping around the place and keeping me up on the phone. It's a good thing you've got friends coming by. You need other human contact besides your mother."

"Mommy don't send me on a guilt trip. I said I'll come by and get you tomorrow, and we'll have a nice mother-daughter dinner okay?"

"Whatever you say. I'm not livin' on your promises because you said the same thing yesterday. Now its tomorrow and you're sayin' the same thing again."

"No mommy for real, for real, I'll be there tomorrow. I gotta go, I got Five-Oh on my ass."

"Get yourself one o' them no-hands jammy."

"Yes mom got to go, bye."

"Drive safely, Lindsay. I'll talk with you tomorrow."

Lindsay stepped on the gas in her haste to get home. It was a good thing she had done what she did, even though Squeeze was kinda angry at least she got to see his ass. He was angry as fuck, she thought as she maneuvered the car.

It had been a good trip because she was sure Squeeze wasn't dead and he would be coming through later tonight. She was sure of that. He always come and see her when she did something wrong.

It was always worth the make-up after he had shouted her down and scolded her. After that he would spank her naked ass with his bare hands. Lindsay smiled and pumped the radio volume. Lindsay thought about how she loved the sting his big hand would cause. She sang along to a remix by Mario featuring T.I. and Jada Kiss. Lindsay blasted the speakers of her car loudly as she chanted along.

"*Baby you should let me love you let me love*

You should let me love you give you everything…"

Lindsay was in a good mood even though she knew it came at some type of price tag. She felt it was worth the toll. The BMW sped along crossing from BK to Queens, Lindsay mentally counting down the hours before she would see Squeeze. Before she realized, Lindsay traveling exclusively in a state of elation reached her apartment building. She guided the car into a parking space, raced out the parking lot and skipped onto the elevator whistling happily.

There was pep in her step and a smile from ear to ear, which she shared with neighbors walking by. In the lobby, she saw a face that was familiar. It was Malik's cousin. Strange, Lindsay thought.

"What're you doing round here?" She asked and tried to hug the teen. He looked at her but didn't answer then he backed away. Lindsay moved on. Maybe the jerky boy knows someone in this building. He was nervous, like I caught him creepin' or sump'n. Their family is so large that they be knowing people from all over the city, Lindsay thought and kept moving.

She walked to her apartment and opened the door. Her whole body shook like she had just seen a ghost. Lindsay rushed to try to get back out the door. The teenage boy she'd passed in the lobby was standing outside her door. He pushed her back inside the apartment and yelled.

"This da bitch who set up Malik. This bitch is Squeeze's down-bitch."

Lindsay heard the door slam and the teenager speaking but did not understand much of what was said. Even though it was all Spanish, she was sure she heard him say the name Squeeze. In a hot New York minute, it dawned on her that this was some type of a setup and she could be a victim. She looked into the face of the guy who answered. He was smiling as he spoke.

"Really, not bad. Too bad this girl is pretty. But that bastard Squeeze must die and if she has to die also, then so be it."

Again Lindsay didn't understand what was being said. But she heard Squeeze's name dropped. What could they want; what was this about? She dared to ask.

"Look I don't know what this is all about but you got the wrong place. The Spanish family lives a couple doors down to the left. I'm black alright, and I know people who know some people who can clear up all this mess. If y'all don't get your asses out of my…" Someone pulled out a gun and Lindsay froze. "Ah…there's no need for no shooting," she breathed. The surprised Lindsay decided that it would be easier to be cooperative. "You can take whatever you want. I have some dough stashed in the kitchen. I'll get it and give it to you. Then you guys can leave."

The fat guy laughed out loud and she knew he was making fun of her. Lindsay knew she had a gun hidden in the kitchen drawer. She really was too nervous to even shoot it. Pooh had shown her how to hold it. She'd never fired one before. Squeeze made her keep the gun, just in case. Lindsay gave up on her scheme when she heard the fat guy speak.

"If we wanted to take anything we don't need your

permission." He growled. Then he continued in a softer tone: "We would simply take it. We're just gonna be your guest until your boyfriend shows. Ha, ha, see we got some biz to settle with him and we're having difficulties locating him. Until you came along."

"Why don't you meet him at the club? He's there sometimes..."

"We tried there. Not happening," the fat man smiled. "Sit down and chill out in your nice apartment. Let's get to know each other, maybe I'll let you live."

Lindsay was shuddering so hard she glanced down to make sure that the floor wasn't wet from her urinating. This was crazy. Someone had turned the radio up.

How did these four guys get up in her apartment? Her wits slowly returned and she made a connection. The super was the only other person with copies of her keys and he was Spanish. She'd heard something about Spanish people sticking together. It would be that much easier for them to bribe him and get in. A tremendous feeling of discomfort encircled Lindsay as she realized that she was imprisoned in her apartment.

"No one, nobody is gonna get hurt right. All y'all want to do is talk. And settle some business, right?" Lindsay tried to sound as positive as possible. They all smiled and nodded. She noticed that the teenager from outside, Malik's cousin had left. That made her feel that the guys sitting in her apartment had other plans. There were three remaining, maybe she could get into the kitchen and get the gun. It was in the utensil drawer. Then what would she do? Lindsay wondered. "Just point it away from your body, take the safety off and pow." Squeeze had told her.

"Anyone care for ah...drinks? A beer?" Lindsay asked.

They all stared at her then nodded. This is it, Lindsay thought as she walked quickly into the kitchen. Someone followed her but didn't really pay her no mind after she opened the refrigerator. Lindsay pulled out three bottles of beer and searched in the drawer for the bottle opener. She put her hand on the gun and slowly pulled it out. She made sure she took the safety off, then she bit her lips and pointed it away from her body. "All right! Y'all get your motherfucking asses outta here 'fore I start shooting!" Lindsay commanded. They all acted surprised. One even went as far as immediately throwing his hands in the air. Then they all laughed. "I'm not playing around. Put your hands down." Lindsay yelled out above the music. She glanced at the gun and then stared at them with an evil grill. "If there's some reason that y'all didn't understand me, then I'm gonna say it again: If y'all don't get out right now, I'm gonna...Y'all give me no choice but to bust this shit on someone!" Lindsay shouted above the music. No one budged. They all waited to see what would happen next. Lindsay remembered hearing Squeeze voice in the back of her mind saying: "If you pull your gun, use it."

Lindsay had made the decision to pull the gun out. She had them now. They were all seated waiting for beer speaking their Spanish lingo making her afraid. Now she had the upper hand she pointed the gun on them. "For the last time, please get y'all Spanish asses outta here!" She screamed.

"Or what?" The fat guy nonchalantly asked. "You're not being a nice hostess." He said wagging his fat index finger. The others nodded in agreement.

"I don't care. Please get your fat ass out my sofa and take your friends with you. Now!" Lindsay said as she took deadly aim at the intruders. They must not have taken her serious because the one who had his hands raised called her bluff.

"Go ahead shoot us." He yelled at her walking towards her with his hands opened and then he jumped at her. Lindsay had no choice but to pull the trigger. Click.

Nothing happened. All she heard was the spray of guttural laughter. "But you're gonna need this." He held a metal case. She didn't understand at first until he said: "This fits on the bottom of your gun. It's the magazine. Mira, this is where the bullets go." Lindsay looked even more confused. "This is where the bullets for the gun go." He repeated.

They all laughed some more. Fear gripped her tighter. She now realized that they had searched her place and left the empty gun for her to retrieve. Now they were certainly gonna hurt her, she thought.

Lindsay saw the notebook that Pooh had treasured. The one she'd kept after he was killed. She knew it was dear to her brother and looked at the pages littered across the kitchen floor. Lindsay instinctively bent down and started to retrieve all the pages. She was packing all the pages neatly as her unwanted guests drank beers. The tears finally started to flow.

How was this going to end? She wondered. What were they waiting for. They probably just wanted to torture her. One of them saw how neatly she'd packed the notebook and just before she bound it all together, he shouted to her when he saw the picture of her brother on the front page.

"Is that your man?" He asked as she stared down at the picture on the cover.

"No, that's...He's my brother. He was killed last year."

She said with finality.

"He's your brother, hmm you don't say? Your brother?" The fat man asked in disbelief. "What a small world." He said to her then turned to his friends and started talking. "He is the Moreno we killed. The one who robbed Julissa."

"You gotta be shitting me," one of them said.

"Get the fuck out," the other said.

Then they all looked at Lindsay. Their stare made her nervous. She knew immediately that whatever they were thinking couldn't be anything good. They all converged on the notebook and each took it in hand and further examined it.

"Read a little sump'n, sump'n, let me see if homey had talents." The jovial fat man said. Lindsay picked up the note book and leafed through it with tears clouding her eyes she started to read too low at first. "Ah you don't have to be scared of us. I told you we don't wanna hurt you. Go ahead read."

Lindsay silently cursed the day she'd kept the notebook. She cleared her throat and began to read as requested.

MARRIED TO THEZ STREETZ

I'm walking blakwardz through parkz of knowledge with no iz to my rear. No fearz. Thoughts like vinyl recordz keepz on spinnin inside my head. All dayz paranoira spreadz like poverty bottled juz for the hood. No one getz in or getz out. No medizine, no remedeez I treadz on the edge of the future and traze the path through a maze called life. Trying to figga like a humble solja on what to do next until I met deztiny. Me n my manz scrambling like kidz all from memory, shit we learnz uzi make uz top notch hustlaz.

Now I guez I must have mad time to chill, recollecting how it izz and how it wuzz and how thingz use to be… way, way back whenz. Thiz Pooh hard riding don't even try bringing your girlz round me cuz if she don't fall for theze sexy iz then she falling for my blingz and thingz. Riding in a benz or ezzkaping in a ezzcalaid or rolln on a Range, lifted on dubz. None out there can shut uz downz. Weze bout da dollaz them scrillaz are ourz theze gunz aint borrowed we changingz hoodz like changing houzewives cuz we married to them streetz wit no namez they got our facez on the cornaz our own big facez on them. Blood running outta you iz murder only a nigga with a cut knowz how much it hurtin ya. I'm hip to thiz and for y'all hataz feelz the shellz bounz off your domez running when I blaz my ninez.

Lindsay paused at the end of the page and checked her listeners' expressions. The fat man smiled and he seemed impressed. Lindsay all the time was thinking that the longer she kept them entertained then the greater her chances of escaping or planning a good escape. Her mind was spinning real fast and she had to do everything to prevent it from going into orbit. Lindsay heard as the fat man addressed her.

"Your brother was a poet and only you knew it," the fat man laughed.

Lindsay smiled nervously and laid the loose leaf journal now held together by red strings down on the coffee table. The fat man picked up the remote and pointed it. He lowered the volume on the spit from JayZ's Roc exit The Black Album.

Can I get an encore do you want more? … Hova, Hova, Hova…

The anthem diminished from dance club volume to a favorable living room background. Lindsay cast a worried glance at the gang of three. She saw the fat man put down the remote, nodded and signal for her to read on. Nervous, Lindsay handled the pages carefully trying not to damage them.

She knew her brother Pooh had tried to keep the pages neat. And that Pooh had kept this side safely tucked away from the rest of the world. Most importantly she knew the reason. The others sat on the edge of the leather sofa pretending not to listen to the words which now came in her whispers. Lindsay realized that she was feeling relaxed also, almost comforted by the poetry her dead brother had penned.

They looked at her and tried to ignore the way she chuckled at odd times. Maybe they'd think she was crazy and leave her alone. She wanted to ask what effect the poems were having on them, but fidgeted with the idea too long. Lindsay continued to read scanning their expression as she occasionally smiled at her brother's intended misspelled words. Lindsay saw how they deliberately looked away. They seemed uncomfortable with the lines. She paused and leafed uneasily through pages before she heard the fat man speaking softly.

"Read a little louder," he said in a quiet still voice that made her realize he had been listening all along.

Lindsay was pleased and immediately heeded the request. Her voice rose lusty and loud with her brother's secret verses. Maybe it will spare my life. She believed that the words gave her courage, Lindsay read on.

When first I knew I wanted to be so much like real gangstaz from the old block. They were kingpinz and bozz going hard, sitting pretty on colozzal stackz, gentlemenz working with crazy dimez pozzezzing helluva knowledge with tight gamez. I want to be thoz hustlaz living in the phattez cribz, the smoothz whipz. Hand over fiz, me and my niz trizin' big chipz. Enemz schemz for C.R.E.A.M. that all mighty scrillarz. I want to be richer than the puppet-mizer juggling stringz with judgz and politicianz attached to my enz. Dangling from my every whim no clue on what I might do next. I'll try invezment my cheddar to make my community a little better place for dez to arrez me in. Dirty politicianz juz ain't helping and they ain't helping me grow either. Robin Hoodz for greenz I'll continue to use kings' ransom for poor living. Nah just kidding—I'll use my money to buy more bling. Nice ice baby. Thez thingz take heart.

Lindsay cleared her throat. She studied their faces and felt the power of her brother's words surged through her and brought about a calming effect on her unwanted guests. Two rose, whispered something in Spanish, turned to the fat man who quickly waved them off. They walked to the door beer bottles in hand and spoke and one walked out. Only the fat man and another stayed inside guarding the door. And now there were two, Lindsay thought. The fat man waved his arm.

"Squeeze is taking an awfully long time to get here. Read

some more then I want you to call him and ask him nicely to come see you. Let me hear some more. Your brother should've stuck with that shit maybe he'd still be around," he said with the big-headed comfort of an arrogant boss.

Lindsay did not want to call Squeeze. She thought for the first time in the last month, this was the only time she didn't want him to visit. Her mind was gushing with thoughts and before she read on, Lindsay made a suggestion.

"I've got Grey Goose Vodka, the best. There's Henney, Hypnotic, Bicardi and other stuff to drink," she said.

There were no immediate reactions. Lindsay was about to continue disappointedly reading, until she heard:

"Bring it all out. Yeah, bring 'em out."

They shouted and clapped. Lindsay walked to the kitchen. She was followed closely by one man who immediately started grabbing bottles of Bicardi, the Hennessey and Grey Goose disappeared from her shelves. Then he rejoined the fat man, splitting up the bottles.

"Bacardi for me."

"Let me try the Henney. I'll mix it with the Hypnotik."

"Now she can read all she wants. This will hold us down 'til her man comes home," the fat man said and guzzled.

"Someone gotta go sit in the parking lot. We want to get some dough outta Squeeze before we kill him."

"I'll go. But let me have a drink first."

"Go ahead read some more."

"Read all you want, ha, ha, ha,"

Once again Lindsay heard the name of her lover dropped. She didn't understand the rest of what was being said. She could only guess that it wasn't good. Lindsay was happy to oblige with the request. She needed a plan. Her survival depended on a good one. It was this in mind that she engaged them in some more of Pooh's poetry.

FAKE ASS WORLD

Man I never grew up watching the world created by tell-I-lie-vision, I witness reality. True life-gangster-lessons on how and what to hustle on the black top of my block. Fuck school. I took street classes and learn different ways to set up shops. Lessons about how spots go. How to cook the raw multiplying rock investments extend clientele dividin corners into sections was on the afternoon program card. Mornins spent independently studyin ways to get new custs communicatin wit' eye. No words needed to steer junkies in a herd crack coding.

That made the hood jumpin hot. I mean that rock was the shit and it went hopping mad beyond the hood. I can't even leave the rest without someone's mom annoyin me. Always chasin me aroun bein a damn pest from hell. All for the get high. She cant see herself sinking low. She suck-my-dick in a quick sec if I wink. Women givin their asses. Men stealin from families. Crack is that precious gem. They come buildings fill. Everyone walkin round their heads to the ground searching for what you could never understand. U see them comin scopin you out. Zombie minds on over-time tryin to get sump'n for no thing. Stank smellies threatenin suffocatin in their housin project. Any block you go theres hundreds or more; it was ez to recognize crackhead stroll. Persistent begging for pennies. Unwashed bodies and dirty hands gears smellin like stale sewer. They loyal custies. Smiles replaced by frowns the walk with head to the ground outside the monster reign big time. Get in where you fit in. Runners captains and lookouts makin money. Spent my day dreaming how I'm a get my bling like I'm in the rap game or sump'n. Nice with my ice a true bonafide hustler. I wanted all that pimping in my world cuz I realize at an early age it wasn't just all about the Benjies; it was about how those Franklins added up in the real world.

Lindsay delicately turned the page and watched as they drank. The fat man laid his gun on the nightstand. All the others seemed relaxed by the alcohol or maybe it was the poetry. Some closed their eyes. Her living room became cloudy from cigarette smoke as they relaxed, lit up and chilled. They chugged the alcohol while it dawned on Lindsay that the words written by her dead brother was having an unexpected overpowering effect on them. It fueled her to read on.

I'm grown nineteen and I've attained this consciousness that money makes the whole worl go roun. I don't have to be in school to kno geography and over stand the fact that if you didn't have the necessary capital them financial institutions gonna treat you like third world not fuckin with you. Who want a give chance to a black man with no money? What type of employment you gettin even after finishin college? Maybe I be oblige step n fetch a little sumpn, sumpn startin in the basement if I qualified. Desperately I keep my ones in check. My nightmares are as real as sunlight. I was doomed from the womb ever since the doctor slapped me on the ass my hard knock life began and will last for the rest of time. It's a everyday struggle to learn life lessons, deep down where I'm from survivin racism part o everyday livin. This the last class. Everyday I awake it becomes more difficult to breathe. Feel like I cant help myself I gotta fight cause those in power the one in charge at kapitalistik AmeriKa be doing everythin to keep the Poor man down. Early I could remember the riches seduced me. I was a shortie on the road to the riches doing what I want and fell in love and commit to the streets. Nobody is gonna tell me how to do this. I'd rather die than bitch-up, switch or run and snitch on my fellow squad member soldiers of the street army, Squeeze, Show and Promise, my fam in this war. This Pooh I use what I got to stack chips and I'm doin what I have to before they carry me out...

Lindsay paused as she read from the notebook of her fallen brother. Pooh, the poet had kept a running tale of his street escapades. These were words from Pooh's soul; it was like hearing his voice. She was caught up in her thoughts, studying the reaction. Glancing around her swanky apartment, Lindsay felt the calming effect of her brother's presence. It was as if Pooh was there sitting around, calmly assessing her situation.

She didn't expect too much. Lindsay really didn't set out wanting to accomplish very much. It started out with her just wanting to be there for a friend. Lindsay was looking out for someone she really cared for. Squeeze had done a good job so far.

He had done right by her and she wanted to exhaust every fiber in her being to make him see how much his help was appreciated. Lindsay was well aware of how Squeeze had come through like a ray of sunlight and lit her up with ice, furs and the dopest crib her friends had ever seen. She had given him the opportunity and he had performed way beyond her expectations. She had to use what she had to get what she wanted. Lindsay realized that after reading the notebook, that not only were they in a relaxed posture but the guns were now put away. She saw that the one closest to the door was now completely asleep.

Lindsay put the notebook down. The intruder by the door snoring, definitely in deep sleep. She crept over to where the fat man was reclined. His eyes seemed closed. She stared at the gun and was close enough to see that unlike the other gun, this one had the magazine that one of them had so proudly taunted her with. Lindsay paused but just as she reached across him for the weapon. The fat man grabbed her arm. Oh shit, she thought her mind sped and her stomach did cartwheels. Lindsay immediately reached for his zipper.

"Is this what you want?" She asked tugging at his belt.

The fat man resisted at first but when he felt her nails rake way past the great amount of flesh surrounding his belly-button he struggled to regain his composure. With the gun in his hand, he allowed her to gain control of his dick. Lindsay thought, wow, so small and tried to grab more. The words almost burst out. Is this all you got? She dipped her head in his lap.

"You're gonna have to pull your pants down big boy."

Lindsay smiled. He had to put the gun down. She knew she had to do whatever it took. There were two men in her apartment. One was passed out from being drunk and the other protected his gun as he got out of his pants. She knew that her plan required some brains and she had to be ballsy.

She was convinced that alcohol had only set the mood

and made the time ripe for the execution of her plan. Only two members of the gang remained inside. The other two were outside. The two who had remained were probably the main guys. The others were runners, workers. She figured the fat man was the boss. Lindsay's head-game serviced him until he screamed and woke up his friend.

"Oh yeah, that's what I'm saying. I'm ready for some of that," he said as he approached loosening his belt.

His jeans was around his ankles by the time he sat, he had dick in hand ready for service. Lindsay dealt with both. She let them paw all over her body. Lindsay felt nothing else but repulsion and anger. She kept that feeling as she jerked on one of them and sucked on the other.

"Yeah papi you like it like that, huh?"

"Ahh..." along with grunts of pleasure were all Lindsay heard.

With their eyes closed, they entered into seventh heaven. Lindsay started to lick on the other man's hard dick. Then she alternately sucked each hard much to their delight. After about ten minutes of constant lip and tongue action both men were lost in bliss. Their minds braced for the pending explosion.

With eyes closed and torso exposed arched they seemed to enjoy being prime targets. They ignored Lindsay on her knees in front of them. Head bobbing from dick to dick, one arm jerking someone's dick off, the other reaching for the gun. Still sucking, she managed to take off safe.

"Ah yess mira, the bitch sucks dicks well. For this we should let her live."

"Now that is a great idea...ahh ooh ah..."

"Oh yeah that is the reason homey keeps this bitch on da low."

"Ah...huh... hmm...Yes that's it, mami!"

"What da fuck!"

Too late their eyes popped wide opened when the explosion erupted. Using her brains had paid dividend. It wasn't what they were expecting. The bark of the gun frightened her and caused her to close her eyes. Her intended targets were at close range. Point blank she couldn't miss. Lindsay made sure. She fired shot after shot after shot.

She pumped both of them filled with so much lead that they were still shaking long after she was finished shooting. It happened just as she'd planned, Lindsay thought as blood splattered, she stared amazed at the destruction the gun had caused.

They deserved it, Lindsay thought as she examined the smoking weapon heavy in her hand. There was temporary satisfaction until she remembered one little thing; there were two more men outside scheming to kill her lover. They would be very angry if they found their friends laid up in her sofa spitting up lead.

Lindsay threw down the gun and hurriedly locked the door. Her speed dial worked quickly to contact Squeeze.

"Squeeze," her voice rushed into the message. "Squeeze honey, sweetheart please be careful when you come around. Be especially careful, Squeeze. There are two Spanish men in the garage or they might be in the lobby waiting to get you. They want to kill you. Be careful honey, they have guns." Lindsay breathed into the phone then hung up and speed dialed her mother's telephone number. She impatiently yelled into the phone. "Mommy, mommy there are two dead men in apartment right now and I…"

"Slow your roll. What you mean there are two dead men in your apartment? You told me that you're having the girls from school..."

"I know, ma but it's crazy. I got home and these men, they were in my apartment waiting when I got here."

"You're still inside there. Get out! Get out now, run. Oh my God, child. Call the police. But leave Lindsay, leave immediately."

"Be easy, mommy. Squeeze is on his way here."

"What is Squeeze gonna do when he gets there? He ain't no police."

"Mommy, when he gets here I'll know what to do."

"Are you sure about what you're sayin'? I mean do you hear what you're sayin'?"

"Mommy I think it's because of …" Lindsay stopped short as her mind went into overdrive.

"Lindsay is you there, girl? You there, honey?" Lindsay's mother asked with great concern. There was along pause on the line as Lindsay thought about what to do. "Lindsay?"

"Yes, mother. I'm here. I'll call the police mommy," she finally said. "I'll call you back, okay."

"Don't you have call-waiting? I want to be on the phone. I want to know you're alright, girl. How did they get in?"

"I really don't know. Mommy, mommy, I promise. I'll call you back."

Lindsay hung up the phone. She didn't want to call the police, but she knew her mother was right. I should listen to mommy at least this one time. Lindsay wondered what she'd tell the police as she dialed. It slowly dawned on her that her story wasn't tight enough. I shot two men, but they were trespassing and trying to rob me, who's gonna know but us and two are dead. The phone rang.

"Hello?" Lindsay quickly said.

"Hello 911, what is..." A perplexed Lindsay stared at the phone when she heard the voice of the operator, then she answered.

"I came home and found these two men and now they're dead and I think there are more outside."

"What is your location? And you said there are two dead men in your apartment? How do you know that they're dead?"

"They got bullet holes in them and they bleeding all over my sofa. They look pretty dead to me."

"Why didn't you say that? A patrol car is on its way." The operator said.

Lindsay sat the phone down and stared at the door. She knew the others would either be calling or coming back soon. She wondered if she should leave her finger prints on the bodies. For a minute she felt as if she would vomit but Lindsay sucked it up then searched their pockets and removed wallets, money and gun. She got busy cleaning her fingerprints off and attempting to wipe blood off herself.

She continued cleaning, and Lindsay saw the picture of Pooh on the cover of the notebook. Blood dripped from the photo. It was like her brother was there bleeding for her. The notebook had blood splattered over it. She picked up the money along with the notebook and stared at the book like it possessed magic.

"What would you do? What should I say to the police when they come?" Lindsay was staring at the photo as she asked. She walked to the kitchen sat down and read another page from her brother's journal.

I wake n cold sweat drips cuz I done snitched or sump'n. I wanted this thing to happen but my mother couldn't understand she told me that there was only murder in the first degree anyway you 're gonna cross it that was what she knew running in the streets would cost me. Fast money, fast girls, fast rides all going down in the streets. I was with it. Thats me sittin in that new expensive whip. True things can flip you become the victim. That would be slippin and a nigga got to be sleepin if that happen. I never want to find myself laid up in the pen all fucked up from this bullshit. Madukes and lil' sis cryin, wishin I never chose this life. Or just live ballin until the day I die there'll be a picture of me on the front page 'He's still Peeps' buildin memorial for me candles and all. Everybody cryin pourin liquor out for the fallen. It's not happenin. Not in this lifetime. Yeah I done heard all the shit being popped by haters if you're the son of a gangster then you were gonna true indeed be gangster.

Squeeze waited at the light, he checked his Rolex on his wrist, just a little past ten. He was on his way to see Lindsay to scold her for playing him so close. Then he checked his messages and the one from Lindsay stopped him in his tracks. He listened again carefully taking in what she said. He checked his weapons. The two fully loaded nines were by his side. Squeeze drove on. He felt an uneasiness creeping up to his throat while dialing Lindsay's number. Squeeze squinted in hope as he waited.

There was no answer and Squeeze peeled out, heading to Lindsay's apartment. Checking his phone constantly in anticipation of her call, Squeeze cursed under his breath. He was close and he could feel his hands go clammy. He pulled over about a block from Lindsay's apartment building. Squeeze fixed the weapons in his waistband and walked looking both ways. Standing across the street he dialed Lindsay's digits one more time. No answer.

He began pacing back and forth. This is all my fault, Squeeze told himself. I got her in this trouble. I wished she'd answer the phone and let me know she's well. Fuck it, I got to walk into that building and take her to her old earth. Squeeze walked boldly across the street. He ran into the building and onto the elevator.

Squeeze crept quietly to the door and checked. He used his extra key and let himself into the place. The lights were on and he saw Lindsay lying in the sofa fast asleep. Squeeze walked cautiously through the place he saw specks of blood here and there, no sign of a body.

"Lindsay, Lindsay, wake up," he said shaking her shoulders. Lindsay opened her eyes and yawned.

"Oh Squeeze, Squeeze you're here. You came," she said dreamily. "I was having a dream about us. We were...I knew you'd come, Squeeze. It was like I..."

"Lindsay, Lindsay where are the damn bodies and the people in the garage and all that other shit?"

"Squeeze, I took care of all that. The police came, people from the morgue came and then some guy from the newspaper came. Everyone's been here but you're the best thing of all."

"Baby-doll, are you feeling okay, huh?"

"Never been better, Squeeze. I just knew you had to be here, Squeeze."

"You took anything baby-doll?"

"Only one of those," she said pointing to a capsule case. Squeeze looked at it and saw what it was. "Squeeze, are you mad? I did a good thing you know?"

"I know you did," Squeeze answered checking the package.

It was Vicodin. No wonder she's all drugged up, he thought, Lindsay has been making up all this shit. She probably missed me so much this was her way to get me here in a rush. He glanced around the place and noted that it appeared clean. Then he saw some crimson specks and Squeeze took a closer look. It was blood. Where were the injured? He wondered and turned his attention back to Lindsay. She was still lounging on the sofa. Gotta get her up outta here. This place ain't so safe no more, Squeeze thought as he rushed to Lindsay's side. "You may not wanna leave here, but I think you should go somewhere and stay away for awhile," Squeeze said.

Lindsay was not fully awake. She waved a hand at him. "How many of these things did you take, baby-doll?" He asked as he assisted getting her through her slouchy motions.

"Only one," she answered and held up two fingers. Squeeze saw that she had been also drinking.

"And how many drinks you had?" He asked.

"Only two," she replied and held up one finger. Squeeze scratched his head and helped her to her feet. "Squeeze could you get my brother's notebook off the table?"

"Sure thing, baby-doll," Squeeze answered.

He picked up the notebook and saw the picture of Pooh on the front cover splattered with blood. Squeeze rushed to Lindsay's aid as he saw her in the midst of collapsing like a drunk.

She struggled to gain control of her gait but with Squeeze's guidance they eventually walked out the apartment and were on the elevator. Lindsay said nothing and bit her lips several times. Squeeze watched her flinching but didn't know what was going on. She held on tightly to his arm.

"Do you wanna go and stay with madukes or in a hotel?" Squeeze asked.

"Hotel," Lindsay answered. "Yes, a hotel sounds fine right now." Lindsay smiled. Squeeze returned the expression. They labored up the block and after several near misses, Lindsay and Squeeze were in the car. He quickly found a Day's Inn close to the airport. After registering with fake I.D. Squeeze was able to get her up to the room. "Why were those men waiting in my apartment, Squeeze?" Lindsay asked as soon as they were alone in the room. Squeeze glanced at her to be sure he knew what she was talking about.

"They probably were trying to get at me. Lindsay tell me about what happened earlier baby-doll."

"I caught bodies today, Squeeze," she blurted out.

Squeeze gave her a surprised look and waited for her to laugh it off. There was no laughter forthcoming. He watched her slidng over to the well-made bed and stretch out.

"My first time and it had to be two, Squeeze." Lindsay stated reflectively.

"So what happened? Fill me in, baby-doll." He stated and sat next to her on the bed. Squeeze saw the way her eyes wandered dreamily as she rehashed the incident from earlier.

"I was too through with that old ass Jewish professor at school. He got on my nerves..."

He listened as she spoke of the worst day she had ever had and what had happened after she saw him. Squeeze waited to scold her on that issue. He remembered the main reason he had came to see her was to talk to her about the visit to his family's home. That was a no, no, he thought. Squeeze listened without interfering with Lindsay's explanation.

"I swear I did not intend to come out there to Carnesie," Lindsay said. "It just happened, I left school and like that I was there." She snapped her fingers. "I gets to the crib and I see this guy, used to be Malik's friend, so I just say: 'Hi.' And then I kept it moving. Got in my apartment and thought what am I doing in these Spanish people's apartment? I mean that's how surprised I was. I thought I was in the wrong apartment. You heard?"

"I hear you, baby-doll. So what happened next?"

"It took me few seconds but then I composed myself and I swore then that they were in the wrong apartment. After that all hell broke loose. They said they were trying see you and they were gonna wait there for you. So I was telling them to take their mira, mira asses out of my apartment. They asses never budged. Two went outside and I... ah...pretended I ah...was getting drinks from the kitchen and got the gun instead. Then I just shot they asses and I called you and mommy. Then I called the police. They came and all these people from the morgue and all that. They took the bodies and I cleaned up some of the blood. I was tired and my head was pounding so I took the vike and crashed."

"What did you tell the cops?" Squeeze asked as she mulled the story.

"I told them that these men broke in and tried to rob me. And when one of them left their gun where I could reach it I grabbed it and shot both they asses."

"What did the cops say?"

"They asked me to fill out a whole bunch of papers and to sign a statement. I gotta go down to the precinct to talk to some detective tomorrow. They said I shouldn't leave town – they'll be in touch and then they left."

"That's crazy, baby-doll. You did the right thing, though."

"Squeeze I'm telling you I began reading the notebook that Pooh used to have and just reading his poems and stuff helped me so much."

"What'd ya mean?" Squeeze asked.

"I mean this one guy was so into the poem he was like 'read more'. And the more I read the stronger I got. And the more they seemed to be falling under like a spell or sump'n." Lindsay said and Squeeze laughed.

"You tellin' me da notebook made you able to do all that. Kill two muthafuckas like that?"

"I swear on my dead brother's grave, Squeeze. It was like I had this power guiding me." Lindsay said and Squeeze laughed uneasily. He stared at Lindsay, watched her grab the notebook and hug it closely. "I could feel you big brother," she said rocking back and forth with the notebook clutched tightly to her breast. "It was bananas. They just fell asleep and it was like 'here take the gun and if we try anything just let the trigger go'. Squeeze,

I was so scared at first but reading my brother's poem made me so much stronger. You don't know. It was really crazy, crazy, Squeeze."

"You did what you had to do to survive. You did good, baby-doll." Squeeze said and kissed her.

Lindsay was ready for this and she slipped her tongue into his mouth. He couldn't resist and held her close as he kissed her hard. She reacted by getting even closer to him and giving him a long kiss. Lindsay sucked on his bottom lip. She felt him push her away then she had to let go. She hoped the feeling would last but it didn't. Squeeze's attempt to glance at his watch on the sly, caught her curious eyes.

"You've gotta leave, huh?"

"C'mon you know the deal. Wifey has not been in the best mood and then you was out there. Come da fuck on. I had to pay for that bullshit prank you pulled earlier coming to da rest. Don't let it happen anymore. If you do, I ah can't be fuckin' wit you anymore. You feel me Lindsay? I told you no matter what, my family comes first then you second. I can't be havin you put my family plans in the street like that, baby-doll. That's totally irresponsible, you hear me girl? Shits gettin' crazy n I can't afford to get reckless now. You know my family is important to me."

"I'm sorry babe. I was missing you that's all. I was missing your ass so much. Shit my head hurts just thinking about it."

"Yeah but I told you time an' time again, do not come around my family way. Stay the fuck away. I ain't gonna tell you that no more."

"Babe I was worried. I hadn't seen you in awhile and I wanted to know how you were doing and you weren't even answering my calls. I mean..."

"I mean don't mean shit to me, ahight. Just don't let that shit happen again." Squeeze screamed.

"I'm sorry. I'm soo sorry," Lindsay sang. "I just..."

"Nothing can justify it, ahight. Nothing," Squeeze said with determination. His voice rose and Lindsay could see his temper on the rise. She began undressing. "Don't bother getting naked or anything. Nothing's gonna happen, ahight. I told you wifey been calling me and I can't be out late. I got things to do." Squeeze said as Lindsay continued undressing. He saw her touch her breasts playing with the nipples.

When it comes to sex Lindsay knew exactly what he liked and she gave it to him. Her hands wandered between her legs and into her shaven pussy. She teased, pouted her lips and moaned. Squeeze loved this about her, her willingness to please him. She had the young body, built with a really nice ass. And he loved the fact that nothing sagged and there were no stretch marks.

Squeeze watched and licked his lips as he felt something building inside. This is not what I came to see her about, he told himself and blinked hard as she squirmed and rubbed her breasts and nipples. But damn she is beautiful. Lindsay, writhing on the bed, pulled her hair back and teased Squeeze. He saw her digits disappear into her moistness and she heard him mutter again.

"Damn," he garbled knowing resisting her wouldn't be easy.

Before he knew what had hit him, Squeeze felt her fingers massaging his shoulders and her hot breath blowing in his ears. He could feel her nipples brushing against his shoulder. She knew he liked this and kept it up. She sensed that he'd be rising to the occasion really soon.

"C'mon, c'mon, baby-doll. Ahight, ahight, a little bit more to the right. Ah yeah, that's real good. Hmm," Squeeze whispered as he closed his eyes and leaned back. "That's the spot. That's it right there," Squeeze said and Lindsay kept rubbing.

"Don't you wanna spank my ass for being bad, daddy?" Lindsay whispered in his ears and he could feel it below his waistline.

She laid her bare ass across his lap. Squeeze got a close-up of her naked round ass. He saw his name tattooed on her plump cheek. Main Squeeze written inside a heart.

"Lindsay, baby-doll, you got my name tattooed on your ass. Baby-doll, that's so...Oh man, you crazy girl." He said as his fingers traced his name and around the heart. "When did you get it done?"

"One day when I was bored to death and missed you so much. You weren't returning my calls, I couldn't think of nothing else to do. So I went and had your name put on my ass cheek. You like?" Lindsay asked.

"Oh yeah...ah baby yes." Squeeze replied.

Lindsay responded by guiding his hand all over her backside. She held his hands as he slid his fingers into the crack of her ass.

"Hmm, ahh yeah..." Lindsay moaned wiggling her ass.

Squeeze felt the tautness of her skin as she rubbed his hands all over her plumpness. Squeeze was captivated by the shape. She's got such a nice ass and it's not even sagging. "Damn! Spank me daddy."

He smiled and Lindsay immediately felt the whack of his

hand burning her cheek. "Yes, yes that's it. Spank me real hard, I've been soo bad." Lindsay screamed. She felt Squeeze's hands stinging her cheeks as she writhed in his lap and felt his manhood on the rise. "Oh, oh huh, yes. Yes Squeeze. Yes Squeeze!" Lindsay screamed as her cheeks stung again and again. He was enjoying it and she knew it. This was the best part about him yelling at her. He was always so angry he'd spank her bare ass good at the end. It brought her more pleasure than pain.

Her ass cheeks were red and her pussy was on fire. Lindsay slipped a finger between her legs and felt the heat. Juices flowed and she slipped the digit in her mouth and sucked. Squeeze liked when she did that. He had often bragged that he had freed the freak out of her. She wanted to let him experience a side of her that she told him no one else had ever seen. His dick pierced her stomach with force through his jeans.

She was hungry for him and his dick poked the naked flesh of her belly, and he didn't want to keep holding back. Lindsay twisted her body and began working on the zip of his jeans to find out for sure. Squeeze stood up and his jeans went down.

His total package exposed she was on her knees and kneading his family jewels as she sucked on his rising head. Squeeze moaned in pleasure as Lindsay's mouth became an erogenous zone. She licked and used her tongue to slide up and down the shaft. His dick pointed horizontal and looked as if it would burst at the veins. Lindsay used her lips to toy with the tip of Squeeze's dick. His knees weakened from pleasure and he fell back onto the bed.

"Agh," he grunted as Lindsay continued.

She kneaded her nipples manipulating them to hardness

while stroking his dick up and down. Squeeze was busy making faces looking like he was about to explode.

"Oh yeah, baby-doll!" He screamed and pushed her head down so that she swallowed the entire thing in her mouth. He moaned and shifted about on the bed as Lindsay made slurping sounds with her mouth on his hardened penis. Squeeze held her head down and forced her lips to his balls. She kissed them one at a time and then licked each. "Agh ugh, yeah! You know how to do it baby-doll," he groaned.

Lindsay went all the way downtown. Her hands were massaging while her mouth was sucking. Squeeze's smile suggested it was going the way he liked it. This was the reason shortie was on my side. Squeeze's mind was in blissful blur as Lindsay pulled out all the stops. She kissed his ass cheeks and then her tongue rummaged between his ass crack. This made him howl loudly. Squeeze didn't care. He paid no heed to his cellphone.

"Eat me Squeeze, eat me baby," Lindsay moaned as she lay back against the pillows. Squeeze threw her on to the bed and dived face first into her exposed shaven pussy. Lindsay opened her legs wider and groaned as he licked her where it matters. She was ready and tugged on his dick begging for it. "Oh please Squeeze give it to me. I need it now, baby," she begged. Squeeze did as ordered and turned her over onto her stomach and pushed his hardened dick into her soft moist flesh. "Oooh, yesss!" Lindsay screamed as he rammed his dick harder and harder. "Oh Lord, yeah fuck me Squeeze. Fuck me," Lindsay begged and Squeeze complied.

He grunted as he bored deeper and deeper. She made

it easy rotating her ass until Squeeze slapped her cheeks and Lindsay shook it so fast he wanted to explode.

"Ugh, agh!" Squeeze grunted and held onto her hips as Lindsay gave it up doggy style. "Oh, aah, yes!" He moaned, thrust and spanked her ass.

"Yeah, baby you want it? You love it Squeeze. Say you love it. Say you love me." Lindsay begged but ignored the fact that Squeeze never answered. He just kept pushing in and out. "Oh yeah, Squeeze, give me all that dick!" Lindsay begged in passion. "Squeeze you love this right...? Grab my ass Squeeze. Yes like that. Now tear it apart baby. Hmm, ah yes it's all yours!"

"Ah yeah, baby-doll. Oh, oh, oh, I love thisss!"

"This is yours, baby. Fuck it good!" Lindsay whispered. "Oooh ogh God! It's all yours, Squeeze. Hmm, ahh, ooh." Lindsay moaned. They stayed in the position for awhile, Squeeze shoving his dick hard inside Lindsay who hugged a pillow and waved her ass around so Squeeze could have all access. "Oh yess baby, that's it!" She screamed as Squeeze inserted a finger into her asshole. "Oh God yess!" Lindsay screamed as she felt the head of his dick pushing against the brown hole. "Agghh ooh yess!" She cried when she feel it going deeper and deeper into her asshole. "Ugh ugh agh ahh yesss, baby. Hmm, hmm oooh oh yeah!" Lindsay cried.

Squeeze was all the way up in to her ass and she reeled from the pleasure. "Oh, oh agh, ah aaah, oh Squeeze, oh Squeeze yess, ooh!"

This was what he loved most about being with Lindsay, she was willing to go all the way for him. There was nothing else to it, except she was there to serve him sexually. He had to admit she was better than what he had at home. Wifey would not let him do this serious ass fucking. It would be all sorts of complaints coming out her, Squeeze thought as he rammed his dick hard into Lindsay and felt her shuddering as he played with her clit. "Hmm, agh, oh ooh yess!" Lindsay continued to moan. "Oh yeah fuck it, fuck it!" Squeeze slammed into her brutally fucking her until he fell against the bed and was on his back as Lindsay mounted him and started riding. "You're not finished with me yet are you daddy?" She asked as she began to twirl her ass and ride.

"Ohh ahh ugh do it baby-doll!" He responded and rubbed her titties as she screamed.

"You want this pussy, right Squeeze? You miss this ass, don'tcha?"

"Ah yeah, oh yeah ahh, I'm coming Lindsay quick take it in your mouth and swallow this!" He begged.

"Nah, baby! Hmm ahh yeah, come inside o' me. Come inside me baby, I wanna have your baby." Lindsay said and felt Squeeze's entire body stiffen for a few seconds as she continued to ride. He held her tits as his face contorted and she heard him whisper ever so lightly.

"Oh baby-doll, you know how to do your thang. I love the way you make me feel oh ugh agh," Squeeze said and Lindsay reached down and teased his balls. "Ohh, yess."

"Ah Squeeze yes give it to me. Give it to me, hmm, hmm!"

"Ah, yeah here it comes, baby-doll!"

"Oh yeah, Squeeze you fuck me soo good ah, ah oh yeah, oh yeah oh!"

"This is it baby-doll, ooh yeah ooh yeah, I'm coming ahh

oh yess!" He screamed and she could feel the warm liquid hitting her inside causing her to choke. "Ohh shit yeah!"

"Oh, uh oh yess! Oh my God, oh my God! Damn Squeeze," Lindsay breathed hard and continued riding. "Hmm, agh hmm, agh oh, oh, oh uh ugh hmm ahh!" She moaned as she settled into a gigantic orgasmic explosion. Squeeze watched her face changing expressions as she rocked side to side on top of him. His dick still erect inside bathed by her fluid. "Ohh Squeeze. God, oh man, oh man. Hmm, hmm ah," she sighed wiggling her hips as she felt him stirring inside her.

There bodies were bound together by his semi hardened flesh and neither moved for sometime. She could feel him still semi-hard inside her flesh. She felt all the juices pouring out of her. Lindsay wore a smile of satisfaction on her face and Squeeze closed his eyes in contentment. He wished he could bring this home and stroked her hair as she lay atop him.

Lindsay was wishing as well. She wished she could save this moment for use whenever she felt down. It was impossibilities they both dealt with. Although no other feelings probably ever existed between them. Lindsay was convinced this was her love. Squeeze closed his eyes and passed out as she played with his patch of pubic hair.

He awoke later with his dick hard in her mouth and she playing with her breasts. "Baby-doll, ahh yeah, I gotta get up out here. Oh, oh ugh agh, yess keep sucking my dick," he begged and Lindsay did work.

Her lip service had him up in a few minutes, and he quickly pushed her off, ploughing deep her. Lindsay was on her back and raised her pelvis to meet his long thrust. They were breathing loud, hard and together as he kissed her roughly and sucked on her nipples. Sweat mixing all the time, she cupped his ass, urging him deeper into her moistness.

"Oh yeah! Oh yeah, oh yeah!" Lindsay screamed as Squeeze buried his dick with each thrust. She arched her back, opened her legs wide and settled into the missionary style. "Ah yeah! Oh ah yeah." She moaned as her breathing was labored. "Oh Squeeze, fuck me baby." Pushing up from on top, he did. He stroked her long and hard as if his very life depended on it. He was the piston to her well lube engine. "Grab my ass, Squeeze. Ahh ugh, yeah!" Lindsay shouted.

Squeeze did work. He continued to pleasure her with his dick game. I've gotta come quick so I can leave soon, he kept telling himself. For now this ass was just too good to leave. He turned her over and crammed his dick into her from behind. Lindsay bucked and swayed her hips wild with abandon. He stroke and spanked her ass until he felt the explosion brewing inside his belly.

"It's your pussy. It's your pussy," Lindsay chanted. "Oooh yess. It's yours. Take all of it."

Lindsay was lost in her world of bliss. She wanted to please him so much. She wanted to make him say her name even when he was asleep. Squeeze saw how Lindsay's ass moved. He loved how she wiggled and she continued doing it. Reaching under, she pulled on his balls until he could feel the onset of an explosion. Squeeze thought of pulling out but just couldn't find the strength to do so.

"Oh ooh ah ooh ugh agh ah…" Squeeze groaned and felt Lindsay grinding her body against him faster.

His thighs hitting her flesh and together they made the slapping sound of someone getting their back blown out. He breathed harder, thrust harder and was moving faster when he heard Lindsay screaming.

"Yess! Squeeze give it to me, baby. Give me all of it. All of it baby. Hmm, yeah that feels soo good!" Lindsay writhed in pleasure when she felt warm fluid swimming rapidly inside her. "Ooh yeah, baby. You came too, Squeeze?" Lindsay asked.

"Yep and I gotta go, baby-doll. Wifey gonna kill me. I told her that I'd be back." Squeeze said after glancing at his watch. He picked up his cell phone. "Damn! She done blew up my celly. I wonder what the hell is her problem?" Squeeze wondered aloud.

"You tell me." Lindsay responded by rubbing his balls.

"Nah, no more," Squeeze objected as she put her mouth over the tip of his dick. "No more tip drills. I gotta get up outta here, baby-doll."

"Ah, Squeeze, you can't leave until you give me a little more, baby."

"Nah, that's playing it too close. Wifey done called me seven times already. I gotta get da fuck up," he said and removed his dick from between her lips.

"You mean you can't even spend a little time with me. Remember how it used to be. Before we used to cuddle up and all that. I'd fall asleep in your arms and all..."

"Baby-doll we've been through this before. I told you my family comes first." Squeeze said and continued getting dressed.

"I mean we used to spend weekends together. I even let you have a menage with another woman. Now it's like wham-bam

I'm out. What's really good, Squeeze?"

"I don't know what you talkin' bout..."

"Squeeze, you've forgotten the weekend in Atlantic City with that stripper. I haven't forgetten. She was eatin' my pussy all weekend long."

Lindsay rubbed her crotch and hips, all the time snaking her tongue around her lips. Squeeze looked at her desiring her more than he wanted to leave but he had to go.

"I remember you lovin' that shit," Squeeze said.

"I loved it cause you loved it, Squeeze. Don't you want my body, baby? I want you inside me..."

Lindsay allowed saliva to drool on the soft, brown skin of her c-cup size breasts. Squeeze continued to stare and his desire was stirring.

"All I'm sayin' is I gotta bounce up outta here, ahight? You understand?"

Squeeze picked up the rest of his clothes then hurried off to the bathroom. Leaving Lindsay naked, head propped up against a bed of pillows still rubbing her vagina.

"So it's like that? After not seeing each other for over a month, all I get is five minutes of your time?" She asked as she continued massaging. "Don't tell me sex wasn't like it used to be..." she was saying as Squeeze returned wiping his face with a towel.

"It's good. You're all that. But I got responsibilities. One of my sons just turned six months and the other is barely two. I gotta be around to watch 'em grow. I gotta help with all they..."

"So when I have mine...ah our baby, you're gonna take care of him too, right Squeeze?" Lindsay asked and Squeeze looked at her. His face was in a scowl and she queried his change of expression. Maybe he was telling her something. She considered a moment then added. "I'll raise our kid by myself I just want you to know I'm gonna have your baby Squeeze," she said in a determined voice.

"Look Lindsay it's all good, baby-doll. But what about college, and all that talk about being the first one in your fam to accomplish sump'n than graduatin' from the streets in a hearse? I thought you wanna..."

"I can still do all I wanna do even with with your baby, right?"

"I never say you can't. Just that right at this moment things are getting a little outta control and..."

"And what Squeeze, you can't deal?"

"It got nothing to do with that, baby-doll. I'm just sayin'."

"You just sayin' what?"

"Lindsay, you know beforehand how things were gonna be. I explained my family-situation to you. You know what I'm sayin' is true. And with things being crazy as they is right now ma, I don't wanna make any promises I can't keep. You feel me?"

"Yeah I hear you. But..."

"But what, baby-doll?"

"No, no..." Lindsay started to respond and then she paused and thought for a beat.

"It's something my mother had told me just flashed in my head..."

"Ahight, but don't be kicking that shit about what madukes used to say, ahight? Cuz she came to the club and hit Show. So ain't a goddamn thing she gonna sing that's gonna be worth shit.

Cuz I know what she used to be up to wit Show. You know how Show used to be wit them bitches."

"Why is it always the bitches and all that? What did my mother and Show have? Huh you tell me, Squeeze. Show not around anymore so you do the honors."

"That's why I won't speak on it. Cuz he's not here and if your madukes cool as you always be yapping on about, then she should be the one sharing all that info wit you. Think I am a snitch or sump'n?"

"Nah, you know me? I'd be the last to play you like that. Know what, let's just end this shit right there. You gotta go home to your nice family. And that's all there is to it."

"Ahight, so whatcha gonna do?"

"Whatdya mean Squeeze?"

"I'm saying, is you gonna hold this room down for a couple o' days until the heats off on your place or what?"

"I guess so. Are you gonna be coming through to check up on me or…"

"I might but don't hold me to that."

"I guess you'll see me when you can?"

"Baby-doll stop making things so fuckin' complicated, ahight?"

"You know what Squeeze just take me to my mother's, ahight? Take me to madukes."

"Is that final you're sure that is the move right? I'm sayin all night long you've been switching back and forth like you…"

"A bitch? Why is everything gotta be cuz I'm a bitch?"

"I was gonna say faggot, but I see you do need some madukes tender loving care," Squeeze smiled. "I'll drop you there."

"Yes drop me there like I'm baggage or sump'n..."

"What da fuck is eatin' you baby-doll?"

"Nothin' is eatin' at me. Wait up a sec lemme get dressed."

"Bitches with feelings," Squeeze whispered just as Lindsay closed the door to the bathroom.

Alone inside she turned on the light and it shone bright momentarily blurring her vision. She closed her eyes and on reopening she felt the tears building like a storm. Naked she sat on the toilet flushed and cried for a while. Lindsay turned the shower on and was out after a few minutes.

"C'mon baby-doll, you gotta speed it up it's damn near four. I gotta go see the wifey," Squeeze said impatiently. Lindsay looked around the room after getting dressed, she saw the notebook and picked it up.

"I'm ready," she said.

As they walked out Lindsay's mind harped on how everything had come full circle. When they first began Squeeze and her would meet at hotels, then he had gotten her the apartment. Everything was so lovely. Now it appeared that she was revisiting the past, she heard the elevator door open and walked past the reception desk and sat in the car. Squeeze appeared to be rushed. She didn't want to make this an angry goodbye.

Lindsay sat and clutched the notebook at first but as they started the journey she felt compelled to read from the notebook. She opened it randomly and glanced at the page. Then she stared in amazement at Squeeze. He caught her look.

"What's the matter, baby-doll? You ahight?"

"Yeah, yeah I'm fine. I'm fine. But Squeeze look. Take a look." Lindsay yelled frantically.

"Ahight, ahight, lemme see why you freakin' out, baby-doll," Squeeze said skeptically. "Baby-doll you've been through a lot. You know takin' that vike could've messed your mind up sump'n," Squeeze said.

He took the notebook and examined it. Pooh's picture was on it but the splatter of blood was completely gone.

"Go ahead, that's only mild - look inside," Lindsay urged.

Squeeze opened the notebook and his face registered total shock. He scanned again and again all the pages really fast. He stared at Lindsay saying nothing. Squeeze started the car and then he spoke.

"What da fuck is goin' on?"

"I told you back in my apartment I read it and everyone fell asleep. There were words in there. There was sump'n written there," Lindsay said as Squeeze began driving and gave her a weird look.

"Maybe you accidentally erased the words when you were cleaning the blood off you could've gotten sump'n on the page and clean the words off."

"Then how do you explain that the sump'n didn't destroy the lines in the notebook? That must have been some kinda sump'n if it only erased the words and left the lines."

"I don't know what to say. I mean I ain't never seen the words, you the one who always be talkin' bout 'em."

"So you're sayin' you don't believe me?"

"Nah, I'm sayin' you the only one other than Pooh who knows da real," Squeeze said and kept driving.

They drove in silence the rest of the way to her mother's home. Along the way Lindsay couldn't stop thinking about the notebook and the miracle she'd known for sure was real. She heard Squeeze saying a goodnight in a tone that sounded more like goodbye.

"I'm a see you soon, baby-doll. Don't start, I don't know when, ahight?" he asked.

"Yes, Squeeze I hear you. Take care and…"

"Lemme walk up with you."

"Nah, go home. Take care of your family, Squeeze. I got this, I'm home."

Lindsay got out the car still clutching just the empty notebook. Squeeze watched as she disappeared into the building.

I hope baby-doll gets okay. That bitch fit'n to go seven-thirty. Her mother will be good for her. Squeeze thought as he drove away feeling that Lindsay would be alright. "That bitch was hallucinatin' for a…" he concluded before turning on the entertainment system. He selected a DJ Lodose street joint *Taking No Hostage*. He peeled off as the bass line thump, thump.

Lindsay took the elevator upstairs to her mother's apartment. She used her key to get in and saw her mother standing waiting for her. They hugged.

"Mommy what 're you doing up?" Lindsay asked surprised to see her mother awake it was nearly four-thirty in the morning.

"Oh the police were just here. They were trying to reach you. They want you down tomorrow."

"Yeah, they told me I would have to come down to the precinct, some detective right?"

"Yeah, he left his name."

"Couldn't he have just called? I mean it's too early. What, he was just in the neighborhood."

"He wanted to talk about Pooh. He said that the same gun that you shoot those men with…"

"What are you sayin' I shot them in self-defense."

"Yes, but the gun was the same one used in the killing of your brother. You may have killed the riff-raffs responsible for Pooh's murder last year." Lindsay listened in disbelief to what her mother was saying. It's so crazy she thought before speaking.

"Mommy, you remember Pooh used to use this notebook to write his so-called poetry. Well I kept it."

"So what?"

"Mommy there were words written in it. I saw the pages. In fact I was reading to those guys who were in my apartment."

"What guys are you talkin' bout?"

"The ones I shot. I read for them outta Pooh's notebook. Then just now I went back to read it, look." Lindsay said and passed the notebook to her mother. She examined it carefully. Then she set it down. They sat in the living room without saying anything else.

"Pooh used to write his damn rhymes…"

"Poetry mother, it was poetry." Lindsay corrected.

"Well, what happened to the poetry? Lindsay the pages have all gone blank."

"Yeah mommy that's exactly what I was sayin'."

"Oh my God," her mother shouted.

"Mommy, the words were so powerful they caused the men to go to sleep then I was able to take the gun and shoot both of them. That's probably why I'm alive now. I read from the notebook, it gave me life. When I went later and look at it. The whole thing was totally blank. Not a single written line was left." Lindsay said. Her mother thought for a while. "Mommy what're you thinking about?"

"Remember I used to tell you and Pooh that our family has roots in the BlackFoot tribe. Well your great, great grandfather was a witch doctor. He had power to see into your soul with these same eyes. We inherited that. It is or legacy. And you gotta use what you got to get what you want. Opportunity don't come calling everyday, you've got to make use of everyone of them that is presented to you." Lindsay wanted to mention Squeeze but she didn't. Instead she listened to her mother. "Lindsay all that happened was that your brother's spirit, in spite of his death, presented the opportunity for you to avenge his murder. You used their own gun to kill 'em. The notebook was just your guide." She said looking at Lindsay.

"Wow," Lindsay exclaimed. "So the words disappeared after he felt everything was done."

"That's it Lin, your brother's spirit could rest easy now."

"Man this is wild," Lindsay proclaimed.

"Lindsay, I've been telling you and Pooh that we're a great family but you just gotta believe. We can do anything we want to do all we have to do is commit our minds to it."

"I know mommy. For real, I think you're right. We're a

great family. And I don't need no other person in the world to tell me. I see it now. I mean my brother's life didn't go in vain. I gonna see to that."

"That's what I been dying to hear you say, Lin. You're gonna be alright."

"I know mommy, I know," Lindsay said as she stared at the notebook with Pooh's picture on the front. Now Lindsay really understood. "I gotta call Squeeze and tell him. He doesn't have to worry about those guys who shot Pooh, I took care of them."

"Ah, there you go again. Squeeze is home with his wife and family now. Leave him out of this. You've solved the puzzle all by yourself."

"I know mommy but he was worried about me and…"

"Leave Squeeze be. If he wants you he'll come to you."

"You're right mommy. You're right," Lindsay said with conviction.

Lindsay's mother gave her a look of understanding. Nothing else needed to be said. She was convinced that her mother was aware of her love for Squeeze and probably about their relationship. Lindsay gave her mother a hug.

"You know my great, great grandfather when he was captured and put to death he was able to escape even death through his strong commitment…"

Lindsay had heard the story before but now she listened with pride as her mother related the tale of her lineage. She wished that she and Squeeze would start such a tradition. She was sure that it wouldn't happen unless he got her pregnant this time. Lindsay felt she wouldn't see Squeeze for a minute. You get in where you fit in, she thought.

Squeeze drove back to Canarsie with only one thought: be as nice as possible to wifey. He had made up his mind to lie to keep her mouth shut. I could use the break Squeeze thought as he pulled up in the driveway and got out of the car. No need to put this bitch in the garage, he thought.

He walked to the front door and immediately sensed that something was dead wrong. The front door was left ajar. Squeeze could see on the inside and pulled out the guns he had been carrying. He pushed the door and walked inside. Squeeze dropped the guns and stared at his house. The whole grisly scene made him want to puke. The putrid odor wasn't the only thing that was foul.

"Oh man, oh man. Oh fuck! What da fuck! This is..." Squeeze couldn't complete the thought. He fell to his knees devastated by what he witnessed. "Oh what da fuck man, why? Why?" Squeeze looked around and tears came to his eyes.

His wifey was naked and strapped to the door. She had been stabbed numerous times. His two sons had also been killed. They were left stabbed and hanging from the door. His mother in law lay dead with a bullet hole in her head. Squeeze couldn't believe his eyes. He wiped them and blinked hard. He wanted to faint but his mind wouldn't let him. It had to be the same people that came after him at Lindsay's. He tried to think but couldn't support himself and fell apart in tears. "Oh no, no, no! This is fucked up. This is so…" Squeeze continued to look and cried.

He took the bodies down from the door. They were pinned up with a set of kitchen knives. His baby boys had both been stabbed several times. After he'd removed their bodies from the door, he contemplated their remains. Wifey lay naked and chopped up near the bedroom door. His eyes soaked with tears Squeeze laid each bloody mass next to the other. His clothes and hands were covered in his family's blood when he was finished. How could anyone do this? Murder his two sons. They were only babies he thought as he glanced at their bloody remains. His whole family destroyed, wiped out and now there was nothing else now but to die.

Squeeze picked up the guns and walked aimlessly from room to room. He did not expect to see anything else. The tears came silently. He knew this would not be where it all ended. He was sure someone was receiving pleasure from all this. And he vowed to bring so much pain, there would be no one left standing.

Whoever did this, their family and friends would have to pay. There was nothing left, he kept thinking. Nothing. He walked outside and watched the sun rising, breaking out of the morning sky. Squeeze realized that his life had suddenly changed in the worse way possible. Now it was his move. Whoever did this would feel his wrath, he guaranteed. He dropped to his knees and just like a newborn baby Squeeze bawled his eyes out for his family.

I
MY

79
STREETS OF NEW YORK
VOLUME III

bloody red

ERICK S. GRAY

The stillness that subsided in the Canarsie Cemetery on Remsen Ave, in Brooklyn New York relaxed Promise's nerves a little. He was edgy being back in New York, visiting his baby-mother's gravesite. But he welcomed the stillness, and felt safe there. For a little over a year now, he'd been on the run from the Feds, state police, and gangsters that wanted to put a bullet in his ass.

He was tired of running, and at one crazy point, he actually thought about turning himself into the police. But that crazy thought lifted from his mind when he thought about his daughter, Ashley, and how badly he wanted her back in his life. He wasn't about to give up.

She's been missing from his life for too long now. And he was getting desperate to find his daughter and disappear from the city, leave for Canada, where he knew a distant cousin lived. He knew that once he made it to Canada, he was going to disappear and become a whole new man, while raising his daughter in peace.

Promise stood over Denise Jenkins grave, gazing at her headstone, and reading the inscription engraved into her marker.

Denise Jenkins, loving mother and wonderful woman. Rest in Peace. May 1981-October 2003. Gone, but never forgotten.

As Promise stared at her headstone, a few tears trickled down his face. His eyes were glossy from the pain of missing her so much, added to the absence of his daughter in his life. With his head bowed, peering at her grave, he quietly said, "I'm gonna get her back, Denise. I promise you dat. I fucked up, baby. I lost our child, cuz I was stupid. But I swear on your grave, baby...Ashley will come back to me, or I'm gonna die tryin'. I miss you, and I love you."

After his small statement, he dried his tears, said a small prayer and then trotted across the meadow to another site he had to visit before his departure.

Pooh laid dead for over a year now. Promise missed riding with his homies. They were family, and now only two still breathed and walked the earth, him and Squeeze. He felt that former part of his life was becoming extinct—nothing but memories, probably more bad than good. He stared at Pooh's headstone, and saw the name *Paul Parrister*, engraved into it.

He became a little emotional, remembering that Pooh was like a younger brother to him. Pooh had been crazy, wild, and a killer, but Promise still loved him. Promise started to think of the night when Pooh got killed. He remembered the phone call, hearing Squeeze say, "Pooh got shot." Promise felt his heart stopped. Pooh getting shot, was like telling Promise Ashley was dying—it was just too hard to stomach. To Promise, Pooh was his younger brother.

Promise now knew the truth, that Nine wasn't responsible for Pooh's death. Pooh died at the hands of some fuming Dominicans that night. Now Promise felt like a fool, because that night, when Squeeze and Show vowed revenge, his life changed. Pooh wasn't the only life that ended that night. He wished he could go back in time, and stop himself from making the biggest mistake in his life.

Now because of Pooh's murder among other things, a war was brewing in the city. Squeeze had his hands full. Promise knew that in this war with the Dominicans, many people were going to be killed. He knew Squeeze wouldn't stop until he or his enemies were dead. And getting involved with a war was the last thing Promise wanted to be part of—especially with so much heat on him. But he needed Squeeze to help him to locate his daughter. Squeeze had the finances and the resources to spread out. Squeeze was on top of the world with his club, and other illegal businesses he ran daily.

And Promise wasn't leaving New York until he had his daughter by his side, even if it meant risking his freedom.

"Rest in Peace, Pooh. You know I always got love for you, my nigga," Promise said. He stared at the grave for a moment and then walked off.

He was uncertain of his future. Everywhere he went, he was at risk of being captured, or murdered. He always carried around a loaded .45 with one in the chamber. Promise had become a man who wouldn't hesitate to shoot first and ask questions later. He had changed over the past year. He became colder, more desperate, and was more willing to get his life back in order at any cost—even if it meant losing his life.

Two police cars with overhead lights blaring rushed down Rockaway Avenue to a gruesome crime scene they received over their radios. It was soon to be daybreak, as the sun was soon to free the night giving way to another day. But the day awakened with death and horror.

Squeeze had no words to say to his neighbors as they tried to console him on his porch. He just sat there; his eyes were red from crying. It was hard to grasp the fact that they had the audacity to come into his home and murder his wife and children—his fuckin' children, were innocent, but the monsters that they were, butchered his seeds.

Some folks couldn't believe the ghastly murders that had taken place so close to their homes. They were awakened by the blaring sounds of police sirens coming to a sudden halt on their block, and hordes of detectives and cops flooding their block from corner to corner.

"Ohmigod, they killed the babies too," a woman who lived down the block gasped out, her hand positioned over her mouth, as she was taken aback by the horrible news.

"Sickening, people don't have a heart anymore," a neighbor chimed.

Neighbors stood around the chaos with tears trickling down their faces. Even though Squeeze was always anti-social around them, they tried to be there for him, but he was unreceptive to their generosity. They knew his wife; considered her a friendly woman, with two loving kids and a good neighbor. Some neighbors were well aware of Squeeze's unlawful lifestyle, but they knew to mind their business.

Detectives were asking Squeeze dozens of questions, but Squeeze was very uncooperative, causing the officers to have suspicions of their own.

Squeeze stood off to the side, as he watched cop after cop enter and exit his home. The crime scene was sealed off with yellow caution tape, and various pictures were taken of the victims.

A few detectives were asking around, knocking on door

after door, hoping that someone witnessed something, but all they got was shrugs and unanswered questions, leading them to nowhere.

One by one, the morgue carried the butchered remains of his family out in black body bags, and placed them into an eerie van that sat idling out front. More and more people came out, even the news channels.

Detective Haywood and Daily pulled up to the house, and went straight for Squeeze. They didn't come as rough and brazen cops; they came on the humble; they were willing to help apprehend the monster responsible for such brazen and appalling acts.

"Squeeze, you okay?" Detective Haywood asked, looking down at Squeeze as he sat on the bottom of his porch. His face was buried into the palm of his hands. Squeeze said nothing. He acted like no one was around.

"Squeeze, we're sorry about what happened to your family," detective Daily said.

"Sorry for what?" Squeeze chided, rising up off the steps. "You responsible for their deaths, Detective Daily? Huh?"

"No," detective Daily replied calmly.

"So, what da fuck you apologizing for? You need to be sorry for the ones who are responsible for this. Cuz, when I find them, I'm gonna get medieval on their asses, and it ain't gonna be pretty. I guarantee you that, detective."

"Squeeze, we need to talk," Detective Haywood mentioned.

Squeeze sighed; he wasn't in the mood for their questioning. Squeeze looked ahead, and saw the camera crew to Fox Five news filming his home, and he exploded. He walked briskly at the tech crew and shouted, "Is y'all muthafuckas stupid! You exploit my family's death on TV like it's a fuckin' joke! Get da fuck outta here!"

He walked up to the cameraman and viciously pushed the man down on the ground, and then spat on him.

"Get da fuck outta here!" he shouted.

The cameraman stared up at Squeeze in shock, clutching the expensive equipment in his hand, being fortunate that during his fall, the camera didn't break.

Detective Haywood and Daily ran toward Squeeze and held him back before he could do anymore harm to himself or anyone else.

"Squeeze, you need to calm down," detective Haywood said, gripping the hot temper Squeeze in his hold.

"Get da fuck off me!"

"Squeeze, we need to talk to you," detective Daily said. "We need you to come down to the station."

"Fuck dat! I ain't goin' no fuckin' where! Niggas is dying tonight!"

"Nigga, calm da fuck down," detective Daily shouted. "We can do this the easy way with you, or the hard fuckin' way. Either way Squeeze, I'm tired of being nice, you still coming down to the station for a talk. Now it's your choice. How you wanna handle it nigga?" he said glaring at Squeeze.

Squeeze held his stare. He was aware that Detective Daily was a tough black cop from the hood and meant every word.

"Fuck y'all," Squeeze muttered, and complied. He reluctantly followed both men to the black Sedan parked outside his home.

Thirty-five minutes later, Squeeze found himself sitting and staring at the familiar basic and bare walls of the 63rd precinct. He couldn't believe he was at a police station, while his family was rotting away at a morgue, and the killers responsible were still at large.

His blood boiled as the time passed without him on the streets putting the word out for retribution. He knew Carlos was responsible, and wondered how the fuck did they get to his family? It had to be a snitch in his crew. He reflected on tonight's events, and everything played too close to home for him.

First, niggas were in Lindsay's crib and had held her hostage while waiting for him to arrive, then him coming home to the carnage of his family. Squeeze wanted to make a phone call from his cellphone, but thought against the idea of placing a personal call from inside the walls of a precinct.

Moments later, three men walked into the underdeveloped room. Detectives Daily, Haywood, and another man unfamiliar to Squeeze's eyes. He was dressed in a dark suit, polished wing tip shoes, and was clean-shaven. By his appearance, Squeeze could smell a fed.

Squeeze continued to keep his mouth shut, remembering his last encounter with the detectives, when they kicked the chair from underneath him while he rocked back and forth in it. He was still fuming from that incident.

"Once again, I'm sorry about what happened to your family," Detective Haywood proclaimed.

Squeeze sighed.

"Listen, we know you want your revenge...but that can't

happen," detective Daily chimed in. "You need to think about things, Squeeze, and let us handle it."

Squeeze continued to remain silent, not even giving them eye contact, as he stared off at the wall. He was very aloof toward all three men.

"Listen, shit is getting ugly out there, and the mayor is not happy about what's been going down in his city," Detective Haywood said. "There are too many murders happening, especially toward innocent victims. You had that shooting at your club a few months back, your friend Show was murdered in his hospital bed, and then they found a dead naked woman in Prospect Park a month ago, she traces back to being Carlos' girl. Now this shit with your family. This war needs to end now."

"It ends when I say it ends. Fuck y'all!" Squeeze quietly said glancing at all three men.

"You gotta be a hard-ass twenty-four seven, huh?" Detective Daily said, trying to keep his composure. "How many people must die before you come to your senses? You and your fuckin' butt buddy Carlos are tearing this city apart, and people are not happy. And if this war don't stop, then guess what asshole, the feds are gonna get involved. The mayor wants to treat this war between you and your butt buddy as a terrorist crisis. And if that happens, you know what, it ain't gonna be city time, or state, it's federal fuckin' prison for you and him, and I guarantee, it won't be pretty nigga. You ain't gonna never see the sun again."

Squeeze took his threats lightly, really not giving a fuck. His family was murdered, butchered like helpless sheep in the night, and all he cared about was going after Carlos and his men, and employing the same brutal fate to his enemies.

Finally, the man in the dark suit stepped up, and pulled out a glossy 8 X 10 photo from a folder. He placed the picture in front of Squeeze and introduced himself. "I'm agent O'Neal, with the Federal Bureau of Investigations. Do you know this man?" He pointed to the picture on the folder.

Squeeze glanced at the picture, but said nothing.

Agent O'Neal continued. "Have you seen him around?" Squeeze said nothing. The picture was of Tooks, AKA Brandon Monroe. It was a clear shot of him taken in Harlem.

"Once again, Jeremiah Dinkins," Agent O'Neal said, surprising Squeeze by calling out his full government name. "This is Brandon Monroe, AKA Took, a well connected guy in the underworld. He used to be a contract killer for the mob, used to work for the Gambino family in the early seventies. He was top man in Harlem, and ran a notorious gang in uptown Harlem for years. We have a file on him so long he makes you look like Sesame Street."

"And your fuckin' point, agent? I don't know da fuckin' man," Squeeze replied casually.

"We arrested an associate that was connected to Tooks a few weeks ago. He had a picture of you on him during the time of his arrest. When we questioned him about it, he was very adamant. We believe that the man you're at war with and Tooks are working as one, and might be responsible for the death of your family."

"No shit, really?" Squeeze rebuked.

"We believe that there is a hundred thousand dollar contract on your head, and a friend of yours, named Promise."

Squeeze was listening, hearing Promise's name in the mix.

"Jeremiah, your life is in danger, and Tooks is a very dangerous man."

"You think I give a fuck…I don't know no Tooks, or whatever his fuckin' name is. My family is dead, and y'all muthafuckas got the nerves to have me down here talking about this shit…yo, where da fuck is my lawyer, cuz I'm bout to leave out dis bitch."

"Calm down," detective Daily said.

"Fuck you! You bitch ass nigga!"

Hearing enough of Squeeze's verbal insults, Detective Daily quickly approached Squeeze, ready to whoop his ass.

"Detective Daily, please leave," agent O'Neal ordered.

"What?"

"I said leave this room immediately."

Detective Daily gave Squeeze a hardened stare, wishing he could beat the shit of him. But unwillingly, he followed orders, and left out the room seething.

Agent O'Neal pulled out more photos from the packet, and placed them in front of Squeeze. One photo was of a murdered and contorted man that lay dead in an alley filled with trash.

Squeeze knew who the man was, Handsome Pete. But he remained quiet. The second photo was of a woman who was brutally stabbed to death multiple times, and lay dead on her blood stained sheets in her apartment. He then showed pictures of Tara's naked, raped, and mutilated body that was found in Prospect Park, and another picture of Show's gory remains. The last two photos were of men that were torn apart from the explosion him and Show had caused a while back on Flatbush Ave. Those men that were kin to Carlos were the ones hurt.

"How many more must die, Squeeze?" agent O'Neal

asked again.

Squeeze was quiet. The bloody picture of Show was fuckin' wit' his head.

"This war must end, Squeeze, and we will end it, one way or another. I'm here to help you."

"Help?" Squeeze chuckled at the comment. "Nigga, where were you when my moms and I were getting our asses beat by her boyfriend every night when I was young? Huh? Feds ain't give a fuck about helping us then. What about Show, who helped him? And when niggas shot up my club, where were y'all…y'all interrogate me like I was da one responsible, but I got no help from y'all. I'm not afraid of the feds, agent! I don't need no help from you, or anyone else. I'm a product of the street, and I handle my own. Y'all got me in this room, talkin' about wanting to help me… but what's y'all real motive? Y'all want me to snitch, right? Give up information on Carlos, or his peoples, thinking he's the one responsible for murdering my family, so I'm supposed to squeal out names for payback, be da best way, right? It ain't happening. I don't snitch agent O'Neal. You can keep me contained in this room till I die. I'm still a gangsta. And I'm gonna ride or die wit' mines."

Knowing that the conversation was going nowhere, agent O'Neal looked at Detective Haywood and he did nothing but stared back at the federal agent and shrugged. Soon afterwards, there was a knock at the door. It was Detective Daily informing both men that Squeeze's lawyer had arrived and was petitioning for his release since he wasn't officially under arrest.

An hour later, Squeeze walked out the 63rd pct still a free man. He got into a cab he'd called, and when the cab moved a good distance away from the precinct, he got on his cell phone and called some people he knew would handle the business and would take care of it sufficiently. Revenge lived in his heart, and he vowed by weeks end, the city was gonna bleed red from his revenge.

Washington Heights was bustling with evening traffic, as rush hour had Dyckman in gridlock with cars moving at a snails pace. The chilly November wind had pedestrians swathed in their winter coats as they moved briskly up and down Broadway and Dyckman. And despite the dozen or so misdemeanor calls over the police radios, the streets had been quiet for the past few weeks, and it was a relief for the patrol officers, and detectives who had seen enough bloodshed for a year.

Very familiar with Carlos and his crew and the ensuing war, the 33rd and 34th precinct had been trying to keep a close watch on their suspects linked to over a dozen murders in the past year. Rumors throughout the precincts were that the feds were planning on taking over the investigation.

The feds were out for Tooks and his connections to the underworld crime family and the Russian mob. Even though Tooks had been quiet for the last past few years by him running his BMW car dealership in Long Island, the feds were aware that he was linked to numerous figures in the underworld, and had his hands still in corruption. They questioned his niece, Audrey numerous times, but she knew nothing about her uncle's secretive criminal lifestyle.

Carlos and his crew laid low in a concrete basement of a dilapidated bodega on the corner of Broadway and 218th street. The owner of the store was a childhood friend of Carlos, who owed him a favor. He had saved the owner from getting shot by thugs.

Upstairs in the store were two armed men, concealing Glock 17's in a black holster, under leather jackets, aware of the dangers that awaited them. They both stood on opposite sides of the store, and kept a keen eye out for any odd behavior coming from customers. Carlos wasn't taking any chances. The streets were hot right now, and every cop in their district was on strict patrol trying to tone down the violence and lock up every Black or Spanish male that looked suspicious.

He surrounded himself with an arsenal of weapons and soldiers that were ready for anything that came their way. Six armed men kept themselves occupied by inspecting weapons, and talking harshly about previous killings in the unfurnished, concrete, and dim basement.

Carlos sat behind a table spilling over with guns and ammunition. In front of him, was a long outstretched table, with massive weapons on display, from pistols like .45's, 9mm's, three chrome Desert Eagles, and MPK5's, Uzis, AK-47's, and a few grenade launchers. They were ready for anything coming their way.

"Carlos, I got two coming down," a man said over a long black walkie-talkie that was gripped in Carlos' hand.

"Ahight...send them," he replied.

Moments later, two men emerged into the gritty looking

basement, showing menacing looking stares and wearing long trench coats. Carlos smiled at their presence. He knew when paid the right amount of cash, the Anderson brothers would do anything—even kill an entire family.

"It's done," Kenny (the butcher) Anderson, said to Carlos. He was tall, six-two, and dark-skinned with a bald-head and trimmed goatee.

Carlos nodded.

"We get paid extra for the children, right?" his brother, Knocky Anderson asked.

He was an inch shorter than his brother and more unkempt with his appearance. His beard was scruffy and thick, a small scar lined the right side of his cheek, and he was more bulky with nappy hair.

"Yeah, y'all do," Carlos answered. He reached into the draw and pulled out a stack a hundreds.

"Here's the rest we agreed on, ten thousand dollars, and an extra five for the doing away wit' his kids," Carlos said, tossing the brothers the cash.

After the deed was done, the brothers got the price they had agreed on up front, the ten thousand, and then another fifteen thousand after the hit was done.

Kenny caught the cash in his hand and smiled at his brother. "Nice doin' biz with you," he said.

"Tell me, did his bitch scream?" Carlos asked with a chuckle.

Kenny looked at him and smiled. "We raped that bitch in front of her children, then murdered that cunt-bitch while her kids watched, took real good care of her momma too."

"Good."

"Anything else you need done?" Knocky asked.

"I'll contact y'all," Carlos said waving his arm.

Both brothers nodded and walked away twenty-five thousand dollars richer. They both planned to spend their small fortune on women, drugs, and liquor.

After the brothers left, Carlos sat back and thought about his girl, Tara. This murder was revenge for brutally murdering her and leaving her naked, battered body in Prospect Park. Carlos felt satisfied that the brothers had finally gotten to Squeeze's family. He felt no remorse for the brothers' action. It was war, and during war, innocent victims got caught in the crossfire. Carlos sent out the message that he was close, and Squeeze was touchable.

"Carlos, you got a phone call," Manny announced.

"Who da fuck is it?"

"Tooks' asking for you."

Carlos took the call.

"Yeah?"

"Nigga, what part of being inconspicuous don't you understand?" Tooks asked, being furious about hearing the murders of Squeeze's family on the news.

"I did what I had to do," Carlos nonchalantly replied. "Revenge for Tara's death."

"Carlos, a hit like that is going to bring in the feds. You don't murder a man's family."

"I don't give a fuck, Tooks. The puta killed my little brother, my cousin, and my girl. Nigga - I had to return da favor. Why the fuck you trippin'? It can't be traced back to you."

"Carlos, that ain't the point, you want Squeeze, you come

at him smart, not like some brute fuckin' spick. You're drawing too much heat on yourself."

"I do me, Tooks...fuck you, this conversation is over," Carlos said, hanging up.

He knew it was wrong to hang up on Tooks, but his temper got the best of him, and he didn't like Tooks calling him a spick.

"Carlos, what was that about? What did Tooks have to say?" Miguel asked.

"Manny, if that nigga calls back, I ain't fuckin' here."

"You sure?" Manny asked, knowing how extreme Tooks' reputation was. "We don't need no problems with him."

"We ain't gonna have no problems. Shit's taken care of," Carlos replied.

Manny shrugged his shoulders and walked away.

Carlos sat back in his chair, feeling like the infamous Tony Montana. He was Scarface with an Uzi in his hand, ready for anything that came his way. His expression was menacing, and he knew that the future was definitely going to bring about more bloodshed than the city had even seen before. He wanted a reputation. He wanted power, respect and most of all he wanted revenge.

Lindsay sat in her mother's crib quietly with her thoughts running wild about Squeeze. It had been twenty-four hours since she had heard from him and she missed him so much. Tears began trickling down her soft sleek brown skin when she thought of Squeeze's life being endangered. He had too many enemies, and it was a close call at her crib, but fortunately for her, she had taken care of the situation before they could harm Squeeze.

It was the first time that she killed a man and the sound of the gun going off in her hand still flashed in her mind. The bodies of the two men dead in her apartment gave her cold chills long into the night. She told herself that the shooting was justified because they were going to kill her boo and probably her too. The dire incident lingered in her mind.

She took comfort on her mother's plush couch in the dark and thought about her brother Pooh, too. She felt that he was still protecting his baby sister from the afterlife; which had allowed her to escape unscathed.

"Lindsay, you okay?" her mother asked from the dark hallway.

"Yeah, I'm okay," she mumbled.

"You still thinking about what happened last night?" her mother asked.

"If he would have come to see me, they would have killed him. I killed those men for him. I love him, mommy."

Her mother sighed and took a seat next to her daughter and slowly embraced the distraught Lindsay into her embrace.

"Baby, men like Squeeze, they don't last too long on this earth…they gonna end up either in two places, jail, or in the grave. You got to try to let him go. I know it's hard, but the more you go on with this, the more it's going to hurt you. I see it's tearing you apart Lindsay. And think smart about your situation, he already has a family, so don't put yourself second for any man, especially when he only sees you as an option, not his main squeeze. Baby, you're a beautiful young woman, and you deserve better. Your brother would have wanted that for you. You don't belong with men like Squeeze. Your brother knew it too, that's why he kept a close eye on you and the men you dated. Oh, God, I miss that boy," she proclaimed. "He was hardheaded, but he was so talented with the pen. Paul wasted his gift for writing, for the streets."

The room fell quiet for a moment, as both women reminisced about Pooh and his crazy way of life.

"Baby, you want some hot chocolate or tea?" her mother asked.

"Yeah, that would be nice."

Donna AKA Misty, stood up and smiled down at her daughter. "It's too dark in here, turn on the T.V and let's catch up on current events or something," she said, reaching for the remote on the coffee table.

She turned to channel five news. The breaking news that flashed across the T.V monitor caught both ladies' attention.

"Mama, I know that house…turn it up," she shouted.

She quickly turned up the volume, and they both heard the news reporter broadcast information to the city and state about a family being murdered in Canarsie, Brooklyn.

"…So far, police have no eyewitnesses or any suspects linked to the ghastly murders of a mother, her two young children, and an elderly woman thought to be the grandmother and mother of the deceased. The four were found slaughtered in their Canarsie home early this morning. Once again, a family of four was found murdered in their home by the husband and father. The father, Jeremiah Dinkins, is now being questioned down at the 63rd precinct, and detectives say he is not a suspect at this time.

Neighbors are shocked by such an appalling act so close to their homes..."

The camera panned in on a female neighbor, and looking into the camera, she said, "*It's really disturbing...such a quiet neighborhood, not much goes on around here. I rarely saw them come out, but the mother she was nice, we spoke sometimes... what kind of monster would commit such an act?"*

"The babies," another man chimed, "how do you murder babies?"

Lindsay sat upright, staring at the TV monitor in horror, hearing the newscaster repeat himself on the slaughtering of a family of four in Canarsie.

She couldn't control the tears that ran down her face. Her mother stared at the TV, her hand cupped over her mouth; shocked that Squeeze's entire family had been killed.

"I gotta see him," Lindsay said, jumping up from the couch.

"Lindsay, don't be stupid. He's at the precinct...you won't be able to get to him."

"But he needs me."

"Lindsay, I want you to stay here in this house...are you crazy woman? They just killed that man's family; it's too dangerous for you to go anywhere."

"But mommy..."

"Lindsay, they came at you earlier, and you were fortunate to escape out of your apartment alive. I won't let you endanger yourself again for that man."

"But he needs me. He's hurting right now. I need to talk to him," Lindsay pleaded.

"Lindsay, they just killed his family, what the fuck you think they gonna do to you if they find you alive and know you're connected to Squeeze. Dammit! I lost one child to the streets, and I'll be damned if I lose you too. Now you stay away from him. You hear me?" her mother shouted.

With tear stained eyes, Lindsay stared at her mother with aggression. She felt her mother didn't understand the love she had for Squeeze. But she vowed no man or woman was going to keep her away from seeing Squeeze. She yielded to her mother's wishes tonight, but she knew that deep in her heart, Squeeze needed her at this critical moment in his life, and she was going to find him and be by his side no matter what it took.

Shacked up in a squalid and sleazy motel in New Jersey, about twenty miles from Newark, Promise watched the horrifying news of Squeeze's entire family being murdered on a rundown small screen TV in his motel room. He knew that it was now or never, and he knew that now was a good time to get in contact with Squeeze.

He checked into the motel under false I.D. He gave the front desk clerk the name Gene Samson, along with a fake I.D to match. He had no luggage, just himself and the two twin single action .45 handguns he had concealed under his black leather coat.

"Damn!" Promise uttered, shaking his head in disbelief.

Hearing enough news for the night, he turned off the TV, and proceeded into the bathroom. But before he went inside to do his business, he heard two loud knocks at his room door. Becoming alert and very cautious, he picked up one of the .45's and moved toward the door with prudence.

He looked through the peephole and saw a woman standing outside the door. "Who is it?" he called out.

"Baby, you forgot about our date tonight already?" the petite woman, with dirty blond hair and olive skin said, standing patiently outside the door with a luxurious smile.

Promise stared at her again, trying to remember. The woman at the door strengthened his memory by saying, "Sweetie, remember you came to me around nine this evening looking for a date. I'm Trixie; you were in the gray Nissan. You were lookin' for a date and gave me your room number and told me to come around by eleven. I'm here sweetie."

"Oh, yeah," Promise blurted finally remembering.

He had driven up to the prostitute looking for some action. It had been several months since he had had any pussy, and his dick was craving for some ass. Trixie wasn't a supermodel, but she was cute enough to pay for some sex.

Promise unlocked the door, and Trixie stepped in, clad in a short jean mini skirt, black stilettos, gray stockings, and a short black leather coat. Her cheeks were bright red from the cold outside, and she had pleasant green eyes.

"You ready for some fun, hon?" Trixie asked staring at Promise.

Then her look changed from a ready to please, to a quick panic when she saw the gun on the bed, plus one gripped in his hand.

Promise noticed the sudden change in her expression, glanced at the gun in his hand and said, “I’m not gonna hurt you, luv. I have enemies out there. Don’t be afraid.”

“It’ll be easier to fuck you without the gun in your hand,” Trixie joked, trying to make light of the situation.

Promise smiled, and put both guns on the nightstand next to the bed.

“I only like to work with one gun, hon…and it’s hard and won’t kill you when you shoot off a round.” She smiled.

Promise returned her smile. “How much?”

“Since you’re so cute, eighty for everything,” she confirmed.

Promise nodded. He reached into his pocket and pulled out a small knot of twenty-dollar bills rolled tightly together in a rubber band. He peeled off four twenties and passed them to her. Trixie smiled and stuffed the cash down her tight mini skirt pocket.

“Um, I know you’re a big boy, hon, just relax and Trixie is going to take care of everything.”

She went up to Promise, and softly gripped his dick and slowly started massaging his nuts. Promise helped her out by unfastening his jeans, and whipping out his hard dick. Trixie wasted no time and got down on her knees and took him into her mouth gradually, trying to deep-throat eight inches of erection.

Promise moaned as he grabbed the back of her head, forcing his dick down her throat more, causing her to choke. The feeling of a woman suckin’ him off brought him back to the days when he wasn’t on the run from cops, his baby mother was still alive, and Promise was just doing him with the fellas. The more Trixie sucked him off, the more he escaped in his mind to peace and a realm that put a smile on his face.

"Oh shit," Promise grunted, feeling Trixie's thin but warm lips move rapidly up and down his shaft.

His fingers moved through her thin dirty blond hair, pressing against the back of her skull. She took on a mouthful and not once, did she come up for air. She was a professional at suckin' dick.

"You ready to fuck me?" Trixie asked, removing his dick from within her mouth and staring up at him.

"Yeah."

Trixie stood up and began undressing as did Promise. Trixie took off everything and revealed her carefree pasty white petite figure to Promise, hoping he liked what he saw. Her nipples were bright and pink, and a handful. She shaved off her pubic hairs, and her pussy was just as pink as her nipples.

Promise stood in front of Trixie naked, his six-pack was solid, and his physique was extraordinary to Trixie. She became wet from the sight of him.

Being on the run, Promise began working out on the regular and practicing his skills with the gun, almost becoming a sharpshooter. He was modeling himself into a supreme warrior.

"You ever fucked a white girl, before?" Trixie asked.

"First time for everything."

Trixie climbed onto the bed, positioning herself into a doggy style stance. Promise got behind her, gripping her by her hips and pulling her towards him. He gripped his dick, rolled a condom onto his size, and then pushed himself into Trixie, causing her to pant out. Trixie grabbed the headboard as Promise tore into her from the back. Her pussy was tight, and Trixie felt all of him inside of her. She cried out as Promise pushed more dick deep inside her.

Moments later, the doggy style was becoming too much for her to bear. So she volunteered to ride him and they repositioned themselves. Promise lay down on his back, and Trixie straddled him slowly and then began moving her small hips back and forth against him with his dick deep up in her. Trixie screamed out, feeling his shit in her stomach. She clutched his chest and fucked him for fifteen minutes in that position, until she came and he came, and then she collapsed next to him, panting and relieved.

They rested for a moment, and then Trixie asked, "Can I see it?"

"What?"

"Your gun."

"Which one," he joked.

She chuckled, "The one on the night stand, silly."

"Why you wanna see a gun for? They're nothing to play with," he warned.

"I never held a gun in my hands before. I'm just curious to know what it feels like," she explained.

Promise, trusting her innocence, reached over toward the night stand, and picked up one of the two .45's that set aimed away from them. He removed the loaded clip, and retracted a live round from the chamber by cocking it back and the bullet popped out onto the floor.

He slowly placed the gun into Trixie's hand, telling her to be careful, that it was not a toy. Trixie sat upright against the headboard, her arms outstretched with both hands gripped around the gun and aimed at the wall.

"Pow!" she exclaimed, looking excited as she pulled the trigger of an empty gun.

She squeezed the trigger a few more times, feeling the thrill of holding a gun in her hands.

Promise stared at her; a naked white woman was in his bed with an empty .45, pretending to shoot off a gun.

"Have you ever shot someone?" she asked.

"Yes."

"What does it feel like, to shoot someone? It must be crazy, right?"

"It's not fun."

"Are you a gangsta?" she eagerly asked.

"Why are you asking me so many questions? Huh?"

"I'm just curious, that's all. You have an intriguing look about you, and honestly it turns me on so much. I usually charge men one hundred and twenty dollars, but you, I cut a break for."

"I must be the lucky one then. How old are you anyway?"

Trixie held his gaze and replied with, "Eighteen."

"Damn, you're young."

"And how old are you?"

"I'm old enough," he replied.

"I never got your name," she said, still playing with the gun.

"Gene," he lied, not trusting her to give out his information to her.

"Gene huh, you sure that's your real name, or you just clowning me?"

"Call me whatever, I don't care," he said. "I think you

had enough of that." He removed the gun from her hand, seeing she was enjoying holding the weapon a little too much for his comfort.

"So Gene, you in trouble or what?"

"That's none of your business," he calmly replied. "I think it's time for you to get dressed."

She stared at him, then to his surprise she said, "Take me with you."

"What?"

"Wherever you're goin', please take me with you," she pleaded.

"Your home is here," he said.

"No it's not. There's nothing here for me," she stated.

"And why is dat?"

"I get by everyday by selling pussy. I want something different for myself. I'm nothing here in Jersey."

"And you think that tagging along with me is something different?"

She nodded.

"Trixie, my life is in danger. I have dangerous people after me. You don't need to get involved. I've ruined too many young ladies lives already," Promise stated, reminiscing about Audrey, then Cindy, and Marissa, they all got involved with Promise and ended up dead or locked up.

"It's my choice, I can be a big help to you," she said.

"By how?" Promise asked, and thinking that him running around with a young white girl will bring on more attention to himself than needed.

"I know people, I can help you get things," Trixie mentioned.

"I gotta leave from here, if I don't – I'm dead."

"You're running from someone?" Promise asked.

"No, not exactly."

Promise looked at her, thinking how the fuck did he end up paying for pussy and got himself a straggler. He actually thought that maybe Trixie might be of some use to him, it was absurd at first, but he was getting lonely on the run, and Trixie looked like a down ass bitch that probably could hold down her own if the time came.

He looked at her and said, "Ahight, you can roll. But any problems wit' you, and I'm leaving you where you stand, Ahight."

Trixie nodded.

Promise continued to look at her, and deep in him, he had a feeling that he probably would regret his decision.

He told her to get dressed and a half hour later, they got into Promise's gray Nissan and headed for New York.

Bed-Stuy, Brooklyn, New York

Squeeze examined the .50 Caliber Desert Eagle hand cannon that was gripped in his hand.

"That's a good piece of steel right there, Squeeze," Conrad, a local gun pusher assured him. "Dat gun is fresh out of Georgia, no bodies or anything on it. Shit, I don't think da gun has ever been fired before."

Squeeze continued to inspect the gun; it was going to be his personal weapon of choice to put a bullet in Carlos' head.

"Squeeze, you ever saw what a Desert Eagle can do to a man?" Conrad asked.

"I'll find out soon."

"Shit, dat muthafucka right there will put a hole the size of the Grand Canyon in a muthafucka."

"I'll take it," Squeeze said.

Conrad smiled, knowing he could always depend on Squeeze to come through for a gun purchase, especially in a time of war. Squeeze passed Conrad eight hundred dollars for the gun. Conrad took the money with no problems.

"Anything else you need, Squeeze, I got you," Conrad said.

"I got everything I need right here."

With that, Conrad made his exit. Hidden out in the back room of a liquor store, Squeeze felt safe and protected. He was in the heart of Bed-Stuy, around his peoples, and he felt untouchable there. Everybody had his back, and his peoples were ready to ride or die for him, especially after hearing about what happened to his family.

Squeeze knew he had to be careful and watch his back; the feds probably had him under close surveillance, and Detectives Daily and Haywood were out to lock him up. He had enemies everywhere. He had two street soldiers on guard outside the room, and he had a small arsenal of big guns spread out on a thick blanket on the floor.

Squeeze had lost everything, and for days, he isolated himself from any outside contact. He remained cooped up in the back room by himself, plotting his revenge on all his enemies. He ordered Chinese food only, and had one of his soldiers pick it up. He was becoming paranoid, and thought the world was out to get him.

He had surveillance cameras set up outside his room, and one outside of the liquor store, so he was able to watch who was coming and going. For the past week and a half, he made himself invisible to the world and his enemies. He only dealt with his man Knuckles, who he knew from Tompkins Avenue back in the day.

Knuckles was a hardcore thug 24-7, he had just did five years upstate for possession and assault. He was a tall dude, six-three, well built, sported a baldy, and had a deadly temper. Knuckles had met Squeeze while they were both incarcerated in Riker's at the young age of seventeen. They had become friends, and had a high level of respect for each other—real recognize real. Squeeze saved Knuckles life once; he stopped a man from putting a shank into Knuckles' back.

Knuckles had been back home for a month now, and he felt impulsively eager to have Squeeze's back in this war against the Dominicans. He wanted to see some action and bust off his gun. He had anger built up in him, and he released stress, by bustin' off his gun.

"Squeeze, you ahight, nigga?" Knuckles asked, coming into the room and taking a seat on the desk.

"Yo, let me be for a minute," Squeeze gloomily replied.

Knuckles looked at his man for a moment, and then said, "Ahight, my nigga…let me know what's up. I'm gonna be outside."

Knuckles left without sayin' another word. Moments after

Knuckles had gone Squeeze received a call on his cell phone. He knew the number, and picked up immediately.

"What up?" Squeeze hollered.

"Bredren, mi glad yuh awright, mi hear on da news about yuh family. Mi sorry, Squeeze," Nappy head Don said.

"I wanna murder these niggas, Nappy head Don," Squeeze proclaimed, with rage pouring from his lips.

"In due time, bredren…mi people ready, and we gwan get revenge, yuh hear, Squeeze? Whateva yuh hear, Squeeze, call… yuh hear, bredren…"

"Ahight, my nigga."

"Keep yuh head up, Squeeze…in due time, dey blood claat asses will pay…I murda niggas fi fun," Nappy head Don said.

"Right now, I need information," Squeeze told him. "Have your people give da word out; I'm willing to pay handsomely for any information linking back to Carlos and his peoples. I want da niggas responsible for my family's death, Nappy head Don. I want dem to suffer. You hear me?"

"Mi hear yuh, Squeeze…it wi get done. Mi gwan talk to some peoples, and get back to yuh in a few days."

"Ahight my nigga," Squeeze respectfully replied.

"Nuff respect, yuh hear, Squeeze."

After his brief conversation with Nappy head Don, Squeeze started loading rounds into the clip of the Desert Eagle. But he stopped, and began crying because he couldn't stop thinking about his wife and his sons. He rested back in his seat, and had a very emotional moment by himself.

He hadn't shed tears since Show's death, and now inside he felt weak. But that weak feeling of missing his family and feeling vulnerable was quickly replaced with resentment and the bloodthirsty taste for vengeance and torture of his enemies.

Squeeze had strength again, between Nappy head Don and his men, and Knuckles being out of prison, he felt whole again, untouchable—but of course, they couldn't replace Show, Pooh, and even Promise. But he had to let go of the past and focus on his future.

Maryland Correction Institution for Women

Audrey sat quietly in the dayroom of the prison, staring at the mounted set near the pillar that displayed an episode of the daytime talk show Maury. The dayroom was thin with female prisoners because most of them were on their assigned job duties for the day earning much less than minimum wage.

She enjoyed the quietness of the room, without some obnoxious bitch hollering, cursing, and screaming at the TV, and having no consideration for those that wanted to listen and actually watch the programs.

Her long auburn braids were freshly done and dangled down to her backside, she had lost ten pounds since her incarceration and a dark blue jumper and gray sandals adorned her.

She sat in the first row of hard plastic chairs that was lined back five rows and six across. She was quiet as a mouse.

Since her uncle's visit, Audrey's reputation jumped highly

in the prison, nobody fucked with her because they all knew that she was kin to Tooks. At first, when she arrived a little over a year ago, bitches were jealous, and hated on her because of her beauty and long flowing hair. But today, they accepted her, and whatever she needed, it was at her beck and call.

Despite her uncle's reputation, she was still humble, and wanted nothing more than to be by herself most of the time, and appeal her case, looking for freedom.

The long hard nights, and continuous crying had stopped months ago, and she now accepted life behind bars. Some inmates who came inside make it easier for her, especially her cellmate who was a young beautiful girl named Nia. They shared similar stories.

She had been locked up for transporting four kilos of raw heroin in the trunk of her car for her boyfriend. She had been pulled over by state troopers two years ago on interstate I-95, and after a complete search of her car, they come up with the drugs. She pleaded guilty in the courts and got served a mandatory fifteen years.

Nia's boyfriend was no support during her arrest and trial. He left town a month after her arrest and never came back. He didn't even put down the twenty-five thousand dollar bail that the judge set.

"He dissed me, Audrey. He left me to rot like I wasn't shit to him," Nia would cry out to Audrey during the late nights they would talk in their dark cells.

"And now you're doing fifteen years for him…niggas ain't shit," Audrey would say. "I was fuckin' with this guy named Promise, Nia, he was a cutie…finer than any man I've been with.

And he was taking care of his daughter, too. I was hooked. We had our thang, but his boys got him into some shit, and he ended up shooting a cop and killing him. So my dumb ass goes on the run with him to V.A, and he talked my ass into robbing banks for him. I swear, Nia," Audrey had said, as a few tears began trickling down her cheeks, "If I could go back to that day, it would be so different for me right now. I would have my life back."

"I know. Tony was always promising me this and that, talkin' about we gonna get married when his money was right," Nia said. "Shit, his money was never right for us to get married. But yet, he was pushing a Benz, an Escalade, and a fuckin' BMW, but his money was never right for us to get married. Now I'm stuck in here, while that nigga is out there fuckin' wit' the next bitch."

Audrey sighed, coming to realization that when you mess with thugs and drug dealers, the other women sometimes get the short end of the stick. She was a prime example.

"That nigga's the father," a woman shouted, staring up at the TV, snapping Audrey out of her daydream. "He was all up in the pussy, and now he don't wanna take care of his fuckin' kids...just like my kid's father," she said referring to Maury's paternity show.

Audrey shot her a quick glance, and smiled.

The woman continued, "He looks like a grimy ass nigga too. He ugly too, she probably be better off if he wasn't the father."

"I know that's right," another female prisoner chimed in.

They both got quiet and continued staring at the show, waiting for the paternity's test results. The room was quiet, as Maury opened up the results and slowly announced, *"Jahard, when it comes to four year old, Natasha...you are the father."*

"I told you," the woman that sat a few seats behind Audrey shouted and she jumped out of her chair, flinging her arms in the air like she was the one receiving the results. "Now his bitch ass have to pay up, hit him with child support, and take everything from his ass," she shouted at the show.

"Shawanda, you crazy," another girl said.

Audrey remained quiet, paying the two women no mind. She looked across the room and noticed Nia coming into the dayroom with another woman. Nia looked over at Audrey and smiled.

Both women made their way over to Audrey, and took a seat next to her.

"Hey girl," Nia greeted, smiling, and looking so innocent. Nia had baby face features, but the body of a woman. She was five two, and was one-hundred and twenty pounds.

The woman Nia was with was well known throughout the prison, she went by the nickname Shai, and was a roughneck dyke bitch to the fullest. Her cornrows went straight back, she was dark skin, tall, with a little weight on her, and looked threatening.

Shai sat next to Audrey, and said, "You Tooks' niece, right?"

"Yeah," Audrey softly replied wondering what Shai wanted from her. Since Audrey had been locked down, Shai had never paid her any attention before.

"I hear your uncle's about to do big things with you."

"Shai, tell him about your plan," Nia boasted, smiling.

"Bitch, calm down," Shai scolded Nia.

"Listen, Audrey, I'm tryin' to get da fuck up outta here, but I need outside help, and your uncle is the right person to get wit' for my plan," Shai informed.

"You wanna escape?" Audrey questioned with a bewildered look on her face.

"Yeah, bitch…I got twenty years in this muthafucka. I don't wanna die in this bitch."

"And what's my uncle gotta do with your escape?" Audrey asked.

"I'll bring you along with me," Shai said. "I've been working on this for a year now, I know it's fool proof. I mapped out everything, and thought about everything that can go wrong. But with your uncle's help, and his connections, he can make this solid for me. So I need for you to get with him, and talk to him."

Audrey felt reluctant.

"Audrey, I got a guard that's helping me out with my escape…some cornball nigga I've been fuckin' in here. I trust him. But my problem is once I'm out, transportation and money. I know Tooks can arrange that for us, and look out for us. You can talk to him, let him know about me, and tell him that I'm willing to bring you along."

"Me too, right Shai?" Nia asked.

"Yeah, yeah," Shai nonchalantly replied. "Audrey, I know you want out this bitch…help me out. I watch your back, and you can watch mines. But if everything goes over easy, we can be home, chillin', and not worrying about this bitch."

Audrey lingered on the idea of her being back home again

and far away from the walls of prison, even if it was by escaping. And she knew that once she was in Tooks' hands, he was gonna take care of her, and she probably had nothing to worry about. Maybe her uncle might arrange transportation out of the country for her, somewhere far from being extradited.

"I'll bring it up to him," Audrey said.

Shai smiled. "Do it, for me, ahight."

With that, Shai got up and left the dayroom, leaving Audrey alone with Nia to ponder about escaping.

"You down, right Audrey?" Nia asked.

"I don't know yet, it depends on what my uncle says," she replied.

But Audrey knew that escaping wasn't a far-fetched idea, especially knowing about her uncle Tooks' past history. And Shai, despite her vulgar appearance, was a very smart woman, who had came up with some elaborate schemes against her enemies in the past.

Audrey continued to remain seated in the dayroom, thinking about the possible idea of an escape. She knew if she told her uncle, he'd be willing to help. Tooks would be willing to do anything for his niece's safe return. She was sure he'd say yes. The idea of him helping her put a smile on her face.

11:45 p.m. Harlem, N.Y

The Anderson brothers sat at the counter of a local bar on 145th street, near Broadway, flaunting their newly found riches. Both men were in brand new leather coats, with bulky gold chains around their necks, and pulling out wads of hundreds to pay the bartender.

"Vanessa, let me get another bottle of that Moet," Knocky called out, causing unwanted attention to himself.

A big-breasted, light skinned cutie named Vanessa walked over to Knocky and said, "Damn, nigga, chill…you had enough for tonight. Besides, where y'all gettin' all dis money from anyway? Y'all are usually some broke ass niggas up in here, begging me for free drinks."

"Bitch, we hit pay dirt… We 'bout to blow da fuck up out dis bitch," the inebriated Knocky slurred. "We workin' for Carlos now."

Soon as mentioning Carlos, his brother Kenny quickly nudged him in his side, indicating Knocky to shut the fuck up. But unknown to the brothers, a pair of ears was listening closely in the bar, especially hearing Carlos's name come out the brother's mouth.

"Yo, Knocky, chill," Kenny said.

"Kenny, chill da fuck out…who gonna touch us, nigga…I don't give a fuck who's listening. I murder niggas dat come too close…you hear, nigga," Knocky said, talking big.

Vanessa walked away. She didn't want any part of the unnecessary attention the brothers were bringing, especially after hearing Carlos' name mentioned. She knew that fuckin' wit' the Anderson brothers could have her being tied up in a concrete backroom somewhere.

"Bitch! Where you goin'? I ain't done wit' you yet," Knocky shouted. "Vanessa, what you doin' tonight anyway? I got cash baby, let me take you out somewhere nice. I got a big dick!"

Kenny looked at his brother and harshly said, "Nigga, you need to chill the fuck out. You gettin' out of control now."

"Fuck you, Kenny...I do my own thang. Nigga, what you scare of? You see dis here," Knocky said, motioning down to his waistband, which he had a .380 tucked inside. "This do da talkin' fo' me."

"Nigga, I gotta take a piss. When I come back out, we gone," Kenny said, staring at his brother in disgust.

Knocky shrugged off his brother's warnings and continued to down the bottle of Moet. Two barstools down from the Anderson brothers, Run-Run, a lieutenant in Nappy head Don's organization overheard the big talk coming from Knocky's mouth, and he had his suspicions that the brothers were probably implicated in the death's of Squeeze's family. His boss, Nappy head Don was very adamant about telling his lieutenants and soldiers on the streets that if they heard anything or suspected anything they were to call him immediately.

Run-Run didn't hesitate; he got up off his barstool inconspicuously and walked outside. He pulled out his cell phone and called his boss.

"Speak," Nappy head Don said, answering his cell after the second ring.

"Yo, boss, I think I got sump'n you've been looking for about da people's responsible for comin' at Squeeze," Run-Run quickly informed.

"Talk ta me Run-Run."

"I got these two clowns in this bar I'm in, in Harlem, and one of 'em are talkin' big about bein' down wit' Carlos' crew. What you want me to do? I think they about to be out."

"Run-Run, follow dem...see where dey go...dem call me back," Nappy head Don instructed.

"Ahight," he said, and hung up.

Run-Run stood outside the bar, waiting patiently for the brothers to leave. Ten minutes later, both brothers exited the bar and walked down 145th street toward Amsterdam Ave. Run-Run followed them, being cautious not to be spotted by his marks, and lingering back a few yards.

The brothers continued up 145th street turned left on Amsterdam Avenue, and walked two blocks up to W 147th street. Run-Run followed the brothers to a three-level brownstone that looked a bit rundown. You may have mistakenly thought that the building was abandoned. Run-Run watched as both brothers walked up the steps and made their way into the dilapidated structure.

Run-Run quickly got back on his phone and called his boss.

"Speak."

"Boss, I got 'em... They shacked up in some fucked up brownstone on 147th street. You want me to wait out here and watch 'em, see what dey do?"

"No, you did good Run-Run. We'll take it from here," Nappy head Don said.

"Ahight, boss."

1:15 a.m. Brooklyn N.Y

Squeeze's cell phone rang repeatedly in his hand. He picked up knowing that it was Nappy head Don calling.

"You got sump'n fo' me, Nappy head Don?" Squeeze asked.

"Squeeze, mi tole yuh, mi come through fi yah, bredren. I got sump'n fi yuh. Run-Run came across two men talkin' big in Harlem, men associated wid dat blood claat Carlos," he informed.

Squeeze sat up from his chair, hearing this sudden information. "Go on," he instructed.

"Mi got an address, W 147th street, between Amsterdam and Broadway," Nappy head Don stated. "How yuh wanna do dis bredren?"

"Tonight, get your soldiers ready," Squeeze said.

"Yuh done know."

Squeeze hung up and wasted no time getting ready. He got dressed in all black, grabbed his Desert Eagle and contacted Knuckles.

Moments later, Squeeze, Knuckles, and another soldier were on their way in a black Escalade to link up with Nappy head Don and his men, they were dressed and prepared for war.

2:30 a.m. Harlem, N.Y.

Knocky sat sluggishly in the torn and ragged couch getting a quick blowjob from one of the local crack-heads. He cared about nothing else at the moment but the pleasure he was receiving from Shelia, a fly shortie he knew from way back. Now Shelia was turned out and suckin' dick for crack or ten dollars.

"Suck my dick right, bitch...if you want dis shit here," he said, holding the vial of crack between his fingers, teasing her. "Shelia, remember you used to dis me back in da days, huh, you stupid bitch! Thinkin' you was so fly and shit, callin' a nigga ugly and shit," he continued his verbal onslaughts at her.

"Look at you now, suckin' dick for crack, you dumb fuckin' ho! You a dumb crack head bitch, right?" He gripped a handful of her sheer brown hair, and roughly pulled her head back away from the dick and glared at her. "I'm talkin' to you, bitch!"

Shelia looked up at Knocky in horror, knowing his violent reputation. "Baby, I just wanna please you," she pleaded.

Knocky laughed. "Damn, you was cute back in da day. But look at you, all skinny and shit...you know it's a privilege to suck my dick, right?"

Shelia nodded, with her sheer hair still caught in the grasps of Knocky's tight grip.

"A nigga got some money now, so you suck my dick like I'm a fuckin' king, bitch. You fuckin' hear me?"

"Yes, baby."

He forced her head back down into his lap, and Shelia

quickly engulfed his long erection, coughing and choking on his dick, as Knocky gave her no mercy, pushing his dick further down her throat.

"Hmm, yeah, fuckin' better... Don't stop," he groaned, having his hand still gripped around the back of her head. "I wanna come in your fuckin' mouth."

"Nigga, what da fuck!" Kenny exclaimed, coming into the room and seeing his brother engaged in a sexual act with crack-head Shelia. "You ain't got no sense, Knocky."

"Nigga, you want some of this?" Knocky asked, smirking up at his brother.

"Yo, I'm going to the store, you want sump'n?"

"Nah, I'm good…I got all I want right here," he said.

Kenny adjusted the .45 he had tucked in his waistband and made his way out the building. On his way out, Kenny didn't notice the black Escalade and the black Denali parked outside. Squeeze kept a keen eye on him, and asked Run-Run, "Yo, that's the nigga right there?"

"Yeah, that's one of 'em brothers," Run-Run confirmed. "But the one talkin' the most shit must still be in da crib."

"Let's do this," Squeeze said cocking back his bulky Desert Eagle.

As Kenny made his way up the block, five armed men stepped out of both trucks.

"Run-Run and Mike, y'all two stay out here and watch out for da brother when he comes back," Squeeze instructed.

Both men nodded and remained seated in the Denali.

Squeeze, Knuckles, Ta-Ta, Nappy head Don, and his most feared enforcer, Rude Bwoy Rex, made their way across the street to the rundown brownstone. The night was cold and quiet, and each man had a deadly weapon concealed underneath his black leather coat.

Ta-Ta and Knuckles entered the structure first, with their gats out, and moved inside quietly. The door was unlocked, and mostly rusted. The only security for the building was a thick corrosion metal chain with a bulky padlock that happened to be unlocked and dangled toward the ground. It was to keep intruders out of the place, but Kenny and Knocky used it as a safe haven.

Squeeze came in after Knuckles, his Desert Eagle gripped in his hand. The floors were squeaky, as they wandered quietly through the dark halls of the building. When they moved farther into the building, they heard moaning. Leading the way was Ta-Ta, who moved carefully down the corridor, trying to be like a ninja in the night, but not being able to see in front of him clearly, he mistakenly bumped into a foreign object in the shadows and toppled it over, causing a loud crash.

"What da fuck?" Knocky muttered, quickly rising up from his slouched position on the couch, as Shelia continued to suck his dick. His .380 was next to him, becoming alert he slowly moved his hand across the gun.

Shelia's head rapidly bobbed up and down, not being aware of the dangers that lurked out in the hallway. But Knocky was well aware.

"Bitch, stop fo' a minute," he told her, yanking her head back strongly, almost twisting her neck. He peered back at the doorway, his eyes transfixed at the dim entrance to the room.

Shelia moved away from Knocky, as he stood up. Shelia remained on her knees and wiped her mouth of the pre-cum he had let lose on her lips.

Knocky gripped the .380 in his hand and moved carefully to the doorway. “Kenny, that’s you?” he called out. “Nigga, answer me!”

Suddenly, two loud gun blasts erupted in the room, both shots striking Knocky in his right thigh. He screamed, clutching his thigh, and dropped to the floor, his weapon falling from his hand and out of his reach.

“Ugh, ah shit!” Knocky cried out. He looked up and suddenly saw five men enter the room with menacing gazes.

Rude Bwoy Rex stepped up to Knocky and began to pistol-whip him with the Glock 17 he had in his hand.

Crack-head Shelia screamed out, but Squeeze aimed his weapon at her and told her to, “Shut da fuck, bitch!” And Shelia did just that, shutting her yap quickly, staring at five armed men in terror.

“Yo, what da fuck y’all niggas want?” Knocky cried out, holding his blood-drenched thigh, his face saturated with blood from Rude Bwoy Rex’s vicious onslaught.

Squeeze kept his composure, even though he wanted to brutally torture and murder Knocky knowing he was probably responsible for his family’s vicious murder, but he wanted information about Carlos before he killed Knocky.

Ta-Ta and Knuckles grabbed Knocky and threw him on the couch.

“Y’all got da wrong man,” Knocky cried out.

“You da man responsible for my family’s death?” Squeeze asked.

“What? Yo, I don’t know nuthin’ about no family,” Knocky

replied, all that big talk about guns and him being a gangsta flew out the door. Knocky knew he was fucked. He just hoped that his brother came back from the store in time to have his back.

"Y'all pick this nigga up," Squeeze ordered. "You gonna talk, nigga."

Ta-Ta and Knuckles quickly picked Knocky from off the couch, and had him tightly gripped by both of his arms. Squeeze aimed the large steel cannon at his dick and threatened to blow his dick off if he didn't give a name.

"C'mon man... chill... I don't know nuthin'," Knocky pleaded.

"I want a name and location," Squeeze said.

"I don't know shit," Knocky repeated.

Bang! Shots from the Desert Eagle exploded from Squeeze's hand and hit Knocky in his knee, paralyzing him instantly. The large .50 caliber handgun almost completely tore off his right knee.

Knocky screamed out intensely, as he collapsed from Ta-Ta and Knuckle's grip and fell back on the floor. His screaming was loud and dreadful, and crack head Shelia helplessly watched as they tortured Knocky.

"A name and location," Squeeze sternly repeated. "And dis time, I won't miss your dick."

Blood was everywhere, and the near sight of it made Shelia want to throw up.

Knocky lay in the fetal position against the floor. The pain was intense, his screams piercing. He knew they meant business. He couldn't feel his right leg, and his vision became blurry. He was losing a lot of blood from the three gunshots wounds he had already suffered, and he knew he was dying.

"Nigga, we can make da pain go away, just give me a name and location," Squeeze repeated, attempting to get some kind of valuable information from him before he died.

Once again, nothing from Knocky as he remained glued to the floor in his own blood, whimpering and wishing for the pain to go away.

Squeeze looked down at him in shock, and said to his men, "Yo, dis nigga just won't fuckin' listen…nigga, why you so fuckin' hardheaded? Give me a fuckin' name, and you gonna be good soon!" he said, looking impatient.

"Squeeze, him not talkin', let me gwan at him, him will talk," Nappy head Don interjected.

Squeeze shrugged and said, "Go ahead, nigga, do what you gotta do."

Nappy head Don nodded to his enforcer, Rude Bwoy Rex, and Rex smiled at the opportunity. Rude Bwoy Rex passed Nappy head Don his Glock 17 and pulled out a large hunting knife from his inner coat. The knife had a simulated wood grain handle, with finger holes; it was 12" long with a 420 surgical stainless steel blade. Rude Bwoy Rex stood over the paralyzed Knocky with the knife gripped in his hand. Hardly ever speaking, Rude Bwoy Rex looked at Ta-Ta.

Ta-Ta went over to Knocky, positioned him on his back and began unbuckling his pants. Moments later, they had Knocky bent over the couch, with his pants around his ankles. Rude Bwoy Rex walked up to Knocky with the huge blade in his hand, but before Rex would continue, he looked at Squeeze.

"Nigga, once again, a name and location," Squeeze said.

Nothing. Knocky was very adamant. "Fuck him," Squeeze barked, and nodded for Rude Bwoy Rex to continue. And he did with a smile. He went up to Knocky, placed the huge blade near his ass, and slowly and painfully began shoving inch by inch of the blade into Knocky's rectum.

"Ah ugh ah!"

The pain was intolerable, and the screams were loud and shattering, causing Shelia to cover her ears and shed tears as she watched in horror the cruelty and malice of the act they implemented on Knocky.

"Talk nigga, talk," Squeeze tormented. "Da sooner you talk da sooner it's over."

Wanting to die, Knocky never felt so much pain, feeling like he was about to pass out and die, he reluctantly dispensed a name from his lips, "Carlos sent us.... it was Carlos." And with that, he gave Squeeze the vital information he desired.

Kenny took a long drag from his cancer stick as he made his way down 147th street to the crib. The wind was cold, and he had his leather zipped up to his neck, walking briskly down the street.

He had a bad feeling within him. He felt something wasn't right. He hated when his brother Knocky ran his mouth like it was nothing. He realized that if word got out that he and his brother were responsible for killing that family in Brooklyn, they were going to be dead, or if caught by the law, both men were looking at life in prison. The money was good, but the karma that came along with a job like that, put them both at high risk.

A few houses down from his place, Kenny slowed up his steps, noticing two black SUV's parked across the street from his place - something didn't sit right with him. He peered at the Escalade and the Denali, and steadily reached for his .45 under his coat. His only regret was that the gun was still on safety and there wasn't a round in the chamber.

"Shit!" Kenny mumbled.

He knew it was bad. He thought, were they here before I left? He cursed himself for not being more observant. His brother came to mind, and the thought of something happening to his brother at this moment, set a rage in him. But he knew that it was too risky to walk up in his crib. He didn't know how many men were there. He knew that they probably found them because of his brother's loose mouth in the bar earlier - it had to be the only way.

Slowly he made his way up the block never taking his eyes off the two trucks. He was waiting and contemplating his move.

He saw a light go off in the Escalade, somebody was lighting a cigarette, and he quickly saw two silhouettes in the truck. Kenny pulled out his gun knowing that every second that passed meant his brother was in more danger.

He removed the safety and cocked back his .45, ready for anything. There was no way for him to contact his brother to see if he was okay. Kenny was at a dead end. He thought his brother was probably dead already.

Having streets smarts, Kenny knew that the two men in

the truck were acting as lookouts, and he knew that his brother probably had already been harmed or worse, was already dead.

"Fuck it!" he said.

He crossed the street, and was going to get the attention of the men inside his dwellings the only way possible.

In the night, he walked up to the Escalade, his arm outstretched with the .45 gripped tightly in hand and started squeezing off shots into the windshield.

"Y'all fuckin' here for me and my brother, huh!" Kenny screamed, firing and firing at the truck.

"Oh Shit!" Run-Run yelled, catching a slug in his shoulder.

Mike ran out the truck and took cover at the rear, leaving Run-Run in the line of fire. Mike pulled out his .9mm and took aim at Kenny, but Kenny never stopped shooting, missing Mike's head by inches.

Squeeze, Ta-Ta and the rest came running out of the brownstone the minute they heard shots fired outside. With their guns out, Squeeze saw the chaos across the street and quickly took aim at Kenny. Kenny never saw it coming. He glanced toward Squeeze's direction, but before he could turn and react, the bullet hit him in his shoulder. The .50 caliber tore through him like a sledgehammer. The blast almost lifted him off his feet.

Seconds later, Kenny was met by a barrage of gunfire coming from Nappy Head Don, Ta-Ta, Knuckles and the rest. Outnumbered and injured, Kenny took off running down the block with bullets whizzing inches from his head.

Squeeze started to give chase, but was stopped by Nappy head Don, who warned him about police. Reluctantly, Squeeze piled back into the truck with his crew and sped off.

Kenny made his way to 150th street and Convent Avenue with his gun still in hand. He heard the sirens from a distance, and took cover in a quick alley. Breathing heavily and trying to tend to his gunshot wound, which hurt like hell, he fell back against the bricked alley wall and slid down onto his ass.

He knew his brother was dead and a few tears trickled down his cheek. He only had one option, search for Carlos and ask for his help. He had nowhere else to go. Kenny knew that if captured by police, his life was definitely over. He slowly picked himself up off his ass and made his way back onto Convent Avenue, and looked around for the nearest car to steal. He needed to get to Washington Heights to warn Carlos, and needed his aid desperately.

Lucky for Kenny, as he made his way up Convent, he noticed a group of young women standing outside next to an idling Nissan on the corner of 151st street and Convent. They looked like they were on their way to a club. In a desperate attempt, he strutted up to them trying to be concealed by the night, and raised his weapon.

As the three young ladies laughed and waited for their fourth to arrive from her apartment, they had no idea that their night was about to end badly.

"Y'all bitches get da fuck away from da car!" Kenny shouted startling all three ladies, as he ran up on them with his arm outstretched aiming his weapon madly at them. He went to the driver's side, snatched the door open, and pulled the driver out from under the staring wheel, causing her to scream and panic as she landed on her side against the cracked cold sidewalk.

Kenny wasted no time jumping in on the driver's side and driving away like a mad man, leaving the three ladies frantic and crying.

6:20 a.m. Harlem

Several Homicide detectives and dozens of police officers flooded 147th street. They closed off the block and interviewed dozens of neighbors, but nobody saw a thing - they were either in bed already or not even home during the time of the shooting.

Word got out that there was a shootout and there were two mutilated bodies found in the abandoned brownstone on the block. Cops swarmed every inch of the neighborhood and tried to piece together on what probably had taken place earlier. They found dozens and dozens of shell casings that vary from different guns. They were even stunned to see casings of a .50 caliber handgun. They knew that whoever had that gun, meant serious business tonight.

Inside the brownstone, the sight of Knocky and Shelia appalled detectives. Knocky had a Columbian bow-tie executed on him, which meant that they cut open his throat and pulled his tongue through it, and it didn't help the scene more that his anal/ rectum was a bloody mess and torn apart from the sharp blade forced into him. His pants lay around his ankles, and they knew he had died a horrible death.

Shelia was shot twice in her head and died with her eyes opened. Cops combed every inch of the place thoroughly and looked for any evidence to link them to the killers.

The media flooded the area too, wanting coverage and

information of the chaotic episode that happened, as they loitered behind the yellow police tape, asking questions and looking for their next prime time story.

"Detective… Detective does tonight's carnage have anything to do with the death of that Brooklyn family several weeks ago?" a female reporter asked detective McGuiness who was stepping out of his black Caprice. He was the lead homicide detective on the scene.

"No questions," he quickly replied, rushing by reporters and cameras and into the crime scene.

Detective Henry McGuiness was a twenty year veteran on the force, and had seen it all from murder, rape, to even a man pushed onto the tracks of an oncoming A train at the 125th street station a few years ago. McGuiness had salt and peppered hair, was a slim fit white male, had blue eyes and a raunchy street attitude.

"We have two dead, one male and female," a colleague informed him. "It seemed they came for the male, they really worked him over good. It ain't pretty, McGuiness." He was briefed as he made his way down the shabby corridor, passing officers on guard and CSI.

He examined the area and the bodies meticulously putting together his conclusion of events that may have taken place.

Detective McGuiness hunkered down over Knocky's contorted remains and shook his head in disgust at what one human could coldly do to another. He looked for anything out of the ordinary.

"I want a DNA test done on him immediately… see if he's connected to that murdered family in Brooklyn," he instructed his colleagues.

He knew that the woman in Brooklyn was severely raped and battered, and Knocky fit the description of the one witness' statement they had that saw him leave the scene.

He then studied his next victim, Shelia, and knew by her ragged appearance she was a serious drug abuser.

"It seemed our boy was having himself a little fun before his attackers came for him," he stated.

He peered down at the crack vial. He knew that there was more than one man that came for the victim because of the different patterns of sneakers and boot footprints that were outlined on the dusty wooden floor.

McGuiness also figured out that they killed the woman because she was a potential witness.

Everything inside was bagged and photographed.

Outside, McGuiness mapped out the scene, stating, "My guess, while they were killing our boy inside, his partner must have showed up and caught onto the peculiar vehicle that was parked outside his resident with occupants inside—lookouts, I assume. He pulled out his gun, fired his weapon at the vehicle, and our boys inside must have heard the shots, came out and shot back at him. He got hit, and ran up the block, that explains the trail of blood up the street."

"I want every hospital on alert for anyone coming in with a gunshot wound. I want fingerprints taken from both our victims. I want some background information on them. I know our Vic must have an extensive rap sheet. We find out who he is, and it will help make this case mush easier," McGuiness said.

"McGuiness, we have a report of a car-jacking taking place

early this morning," a detective informed him.

"Did they get a good look at the suspect?"

"Yes, three ladies in their mid twenties were held at gun point, and he sped away in a silver four-door Nissan Altima. They said he was tall and bleeding from his shoulder," the young detective reported.

"That's our boy, then," McGuiness said.

Washington Heights

Kenny finally made his way to Carlos' spot on 218th street. He parked the stolen Altima a few blocks down and briskly walked to the bodega. He rushed inside, clutching his shoulder, and being greeted by two of Carlos' armed lookouts. He uttered, "I gotta see Carlos."

"Hold it right there, partner!" the tall, chubby man in the long leather coat exclaimed, with his right hand near his holstered Glock.

"This shit is important. My brother is dead," Kenny stated frantically.

The man got on his radio and called for Carlos, who was downstairs asleep. "Boss! Yo boss...we got a situation up here."

Carlos heard the crackling of the radio blaring from the table. He was sprawled out on a single mattress on the concrete floor, holding a .357 in hand just in case of any situation.

He slowly picked himself up from the mattress, moved to the table, placed the gun down, and picked up the radio.

"Boom, you better have a good reason for wakin' me up," he barked.

"We got one of the Anderson brothers upstairs, he wants to see you. Shit looks bad, boss," Boom explained.

"Fuck!" Carlos cursed. "Boom, you escort dat nigga down here."

"Ahight, boss."

Moments later, Boom ushered the injured Kenny down into the dimly lit basement of the bodega.

"Damn nigga, what da fuck happened to you?" Carlos asked, staring at the exhausted and bleeding Kenny. "Nigga, you bleeding all over my fuckin' floor."

"Sorry Carlos, but yo…dey came at us!" Kenny let it be known.

"Who?"

"Squeeze, dey got Knocky."

"Damn! And why did you bring your ass here?" Carlos asked, looking irate.

"I need your help, Carlos. I got nowhere else to go," he explained.

"What did your brother tell 'em?" Carlos asked.

"What? I don't know. I was comin' from da store, saw 'em outside my crib," Kenny explained.

"Kenny, dis is important…answer me, did your brother give them any kind of information about dis place?" Carlos asked.

"I don't know...he probably wouldn't," Kenny replied.

"Probably is not good enough fo' me. I need to know."

"I don't know what he might have told them. I don't know what da fuck dey did to him. I know he's dead, Carlos, and you gotta take care of this." Kenny was looking irritated and desperate.

"Fuckin' idiots!" Carlos screamed. "How can you and your brother be so stupid? Y'all shoulda kept y'all fuckin' mouths shut."

"It was Knocky, he was talkin' big shit about doin' a job for you in the bar last night, and someone must have overheard him...dey must have followed us."

"Carelessness is something I don't tolerate, Kenny. Your brother should have kept his mouth shut and you wouldn't be in dis predicament right now," Carlos said, walking toward his desk.

"What we gonna do?" Kenny asked.

"We?" Carlos replied.

And instantaneously, Kenny was wide-eyed as he stared down the barrel of a .357, then—POW—Carlos shot him in the head. Kenny collapsed in front of Boom, who was not surprised by Carlos' sudden actions.

"Fuckin' idiot," Carlos once again cursed, staring down at Kenny's lifeless body.

"What we gonna do, boss?" Boom asked.

"Call up everyone...we're packin' up and leaving dis place right away. And take dis peace of shit out of here and dump him somewhere."

"Got you."

Carlos knew he had to leave, it would be a matter of time before Squeeze or someone else tracked him back to this place. And the last thing he needed was an ambush.

He quickly got dressed, and his crew packed away the

ample amount of guns they had in duffle bags and boxes and moved the ammunition through the back door of the store.

They rolled Kenny's body into a sheet, and secured it with duct tape around his feet and upper half, carried his body through the back door, and loaded his corpse into the trunk of an idling Ford Taurus.

Within an hour the bodega looked abandoned.

Brooklyn N.Y.

Lindsay slowly cruised the streets of Canarsie in her 645i BMW. She was in a desperate attempt to find Squeeze despite her mother's warnings. She went by his home, where the murders took place and parked outside for a few hours, hoping Squeeze would come by, but it was to no avail.

She then drove to Bed-Stuy, hoping to ask around for him. The day was cold and Christmas was soon to come -but the last thing on her mind was presents and Santa Clause. So much had happened, and all she wanted to do was comfort Squeeze and be by his side. She drove down Fulton Street, looking and searching, trying to remember certain things about Squeeze - his hangout spots, his friends so maybe she could catch him walking down the streets, which she knew would be uncommon for him.

As her gleaming white BMW sailed down Fulton Street, a lot of hustlers and thugs took notice of the young pretty woman in the BMW. She was getting prime attention on the block. Lindsay pulled up to a bodega on Fulton where a group of young men lingered around the store, dressed in broad winter coats, ski hats, trying to conduct discreet business on the block.

All four young men watched Lindsay exit from the flashy whip, sporting tight blue jeans that highlighted her thick hips, lace up leather boots, a brown chinchilla mink coat, and her stylishly long black hair falling down her back.

"Damn!" one of the thugs muttered, as he looked at Lindsay in awe.

Lindsay was definitely eye-candy for the fellas standing out in the cold.

"Excuse me, maybe y'all can help me," Lindsay innocently called out to the thuggish young men.

"Luv, I can help you with anything you want," one of the men stated. "What you need?"

"I'm lookin' for Squeeze," she mentioned. "Do y'all know him?"

Hearing Squeeze's name come out her mouth made them silent. They looked at Lindsay and wondered what she wanted with Squeeze. They knew Squeeze; his reputation had grown rapidly the past year—and with the violence that was spreading in the city because of his name, they wondered if Lindsay was friend or foe.

"Why you lookin?" one asked, he was the tallest, sporting a black thick Sean John coat with long braids under his ski hat, that dangled down his back.

"I'm Lindsay, Squeeze knows me. I'm Pooh's little sister... y'all remember him?"

"Pooh, nah never heard of him," one thug said.

"Pooh, yeah, I know who you talkin' about. He was killed like last year, right?" The tall thug with the braids asked her.

"Yes, that's my brother."

"What you want wit' Squeeze anyway?"

"I need to see him, it's really important."

"I can't help you, luv…you on your own there. I ain't fuckin' with you," one said, turning away from her and walking down the street. Two more followed behind their friend, not wanting to get involved with Lindsay, knowing the shit that was happening on the streets. Too many men were dying in their eyes.

But the tall thug with the braids stayed behind. He found Lindsay really attractive, and was willing to help.

"Jo-Jo, you coming or what?" one of his friends shouted from down the block.

"Y'all go ahead. I'm gonna catch up to y'all later," he shouted back.

"Whatever man, you always gettin' sprung over some pussy," his friend retorted, waving him off. "Leave dat bitch alone!"

Jo-Jo ignored his friend's rude remark, and focused his attention on Lindsay. Lindsay smiled up him and thought he was cute.

"I mean, Squeeze, I heard he stayin' shacked up behind this liquor store over on Bedford Avenue," he informed her.

"Let me see that, please. I'll pay you whatever," she offered, reaching for her purse.

"Nah, nah, luv…I'm good on dat, dis one is on me," he gently replied.

He followed Lindsay to her car, and got in on the passenger side. The ride was fast, within minutes; Lindsay was turning her BMW down Bedford Avenue, following Jo-Jo's instructions. He told her to stop in front of a three-story shop. The liquor store was hardly noticeable; in fact, it was easy to pass if you weren't in search for it.

There were no signs to advertise the location; the windows were unclean, and displayed a few aged bottles of Jack Daniels, E&J, and some Remy Martin that looked like the bottles sat in the display window since the store opened decades ago. And a rusted thick iron steel gate rested in front of the shabby wooden door.

"This is it?" Lindsay asked incredulously.

"Yeah, da boy at war, luv. He don't need no lavish spot indicating where he resting at," Jo-Jo explained. "You heard what happened to his family, right?"

Lindsay nodded. She was nervous. It's been weeks since she heard or saw Squeeze, and she was unsure of his feelings towards her.

"Luv, I hooked you up. Usually niggas won't do this…they fear Squeeze out here. But let me get your number, so I can holla at you later," Jo-Jo said, with his eyes fixated on her meaty thighs, gradually moving his attention up to her well-developed figure.

"I would, but do you really want to get involved with me. I'm Squeeze's girl," she explained.

"Fo' real?" he asked, looking uncertain.

Lindsay nodded, showing him a casual smile.

"Damn, I tried," he returned. "Be careful, ma…shit is hot around here right now. You look too good to be dealin' wit' hood nigga like Squeeze."

"Thank you," Lindsay said, and then she leaned in towards him and gave him a pleasant kiss on his cheek.

Jo-Jo smiled, nodded, and stepped out of her ride and quickly made his way up the block. The last thing he wanted was to get involved with Squeeze and his men. He was a huslter, but on some humble shit. Squeeze was makin' too much noise in his hood.

Lindsay stepped out of her ride, and nervously walked up to the grungy lookin' liquor spot on Bedford. The place looked closed, but she noticed a small security camera perched over the doorway. She pressed the buzzer twice and waited for someone to response.

Moments later, she heard movement behind the door.

"We're closed. Who is it anyway?" a deep raspy voice sounded behind the door.

Lindsay was still feeling nervous when she said, "I'm lookin' for Squeeze."

"Ain't no Squeeze here!" the voice behind the door sharply replied.

"Please, I'm his girl," she pleaded. "Tell him Lindsay is lookin' for him. I have to tell him something really important."

She heard nothing else, just silence come from behind the door. She waited for a minute or so, and then unexpectedly the shabby brown door was unlocked and opened with a high-pitched sound that kind of annoyed Lindsay.

Lindsay stared at a stout dark-skinned man, with a baldy, and with arms almost as big as her petite body.

He glared at her and vulgarly asked, "What da fuck you want wit' Squeeze?"

Being a bit intimidated by his menacing stare and size, Lindsay took a step back and said, "I'm lookin' for Squeeze. He knows me."

"Ain't no fuckin' Squeeze here, bitch! Bounce from this place, before I…"

"Bear, chill out," a voice chimed from behind him suddenly.

Lindsay knew the voice, and a quick smile appeared on her face.

"Let her through."

"You sure?"

"Yeah."

Not arguing with his boss, Bear shrugged and moved his hefty frame from the doorway taking two steps to the side and allowed Lindsay to pass. Lindsay rushed into the dimly lit store, and saw Squeeze's silhouette in the back. Feeling overwhelmed with fanaticism to grab him and embrace him, she tried to calm herself.

"How did you find me?" Squeeze asked his voice dry and impassive.

"Baby, I heard what happened on the news. I'm here for you," Lindsay said.

Squeeze moved closer to her, showing himself completely, just the sight of him made Lindsay excited. He was in a black tank top, jeans with loose brown Timberlands around his feet and a bulky gleaming chain dangled around his neck.

"You look good," she stated. It had been several weeks since they last saw each other.

"Lindsay, who told you dat I was here?" he asked, his

voice a bit more stern.

"I asked around for you, and someone told me that you was staying out here.

"What guy?"

"He didn't mean no harm, Squeeze...he was just helping me out, baby."

Squeeze stepped up to her and tightly grabbed her forearm, glaring at her as he twisted her arm back.

"Ah, Squeeze stop, you're hurting me," she cried out.

"Who da fuck told you that I was here?" he sternly demanded.

"Baby, what's wrong with you? I missed you."

Squeeze still gripped her forearm strongly, doubting her true reasons for being here. He was even paranoid enough to think that Lindsay had set him up, and that she was behind the plot to have his family killed. The war between him and Carlos had him mistrustful about everyone—even close friends. He glared down at Lindsay and shouted, "Give me his fuckin' name! Da nigga that ratted me out to here."

Shocked and scared, Lindsay didn't know what to do or what to believe. She never saw him in that frame of mind before. Tears trickled down her cheeks, as she struggled to free herself from Squeeze's tight grip. She looked at Squeeze and uttered, "I'm pregnant!"

"What?"

"I'm fuckin' pregnant Squeeze, and it's your baby," she loudly repeated. "I found out a week after that incident in my apartment."

Squeeze stared at her and gradually loosened his grip

around her forearm.

"Baby, what's wrong with you? I came lookin' for you because I miss you, and love you so much. I want to be by your side. I heard what happened to your family. I wanna help," she proclaimed.

"You shouldn't have come here, Lindsay. It's not safe for you here."

"I don't care. You mean so much to me, Squeeze. I think about you everyday. And I'm carrying your child inside of me. I had to tell you," she said, walking up to him and hugged him.

Squeeze looked unconcerned as Lindsay hugged him with so much passion.

"I love you," she said. "Hold me."

"You know I'm at war," he stated.

"I don't care. I'm not leaving you, baby."

Looking nonchalant, Squeeze looked at Lindsay, and said, "I'm sorry if I hurt you."

"Baby, you didn't hurt me. I understand what you're going through. I'm definitely here for you."

Bear stood from a distance and watched the beautiful Lindsay state her love for Squeeze. He had a cold heart, and murdered many men in his thirty-five years on earth, and he knew a woman couldn't be trusted. He figured they were too weak and always got in the way of things.

Lindsay continued to show her love for Squeeze. She began kissing him on his neck and confessed that she wanted to fuck him right on the spot. She told him she was horny, and missed him so much.

"Bear, give me a minute," Squeeze told his enforcer, and

walked with Lindsay into the back room.

Watching them disappear into the back room, Bear muttered to himself, “Fuckin’ bitch!”

Inside the bare concrete room that housed dozens of guns and ammunition, Lindsay pushed Squeeze against the table and began shedding her clothing. She slowly came out of everything and continued to seduce Squeeze as she unzipped his jeans, pulled out his dick and began stroking him gently. Squeeze moaned, feeling Lindsay’s soft, warm hand wrapped around his dick.

“It’s our baby, Squeeze. We can start over,” Lindsay quietly whispered in his ear, moving her hand up and down his hard shaft. “We can start a new life together. Just you and me, I don’t want you to die.”

Squeeze remained quiet as Lindsay removed his bulky chain and his tank top, and then she had him shirtless. She began sucking on his nipples and fondling his erection. It had been weeks since he had fucked, and the temptation Lindsay represented made him forget about his enemies for a brief moment.

“Make love to me, Squeeze. Please. Do me right,” Lindsay passionately said. “I want you to fuck me. I wanna take care of you and make you feel good.”

Lindsay was drop dead beautiful. Her buck-naked round ass shone gleaming with anticipation. She stepped back from Squeeze a few feet, and allowed him to take in her beauty and firm figure. She quickly ran her hand through her long black sensuous hair and smiled.

She approached Squeeze again, and slowly wrapped her arms around him, bringing her lips close to his for a kiss. Squeeze gently pushed her away from him, which was followed by a, "Go home, Lindsay. You don't belong here."

Lindsay looked at Squeeze with uncertainty. "You don't want me? I'm having your baby, and you don't want me?" she asked, her voice discouraged.

"Your brother didn't want dis for you. You're in school, where you belong, not hangin' on to some gangsta," he explained.

"But I'm pregnant by you."

"I'm sorry about that."

"Sorry?" She looked like she was about to cry. "How can you be sorry?"

"I already lost a family to dis street shit, Lindsay; they're dead because of me..."

"But we can start a whole new family, together, Squeeze.... just you and me."

"I don't want another family!" Squeeze shouted, startling Lindsay. "Dis me, Lindsay, a gangsta, a thug. I hurt and kill people. And it's not gonna get better. It's gonna get worse. I won't be able to live with myself if anything happens to you. I owe it to Pooh to keep you away from what's goin' on. Pooh's dead because he followed me. Show's dead because he was my right hand. And Promise is on the run because he had my back. Both my families are gone because of da streets."

"But baby...let's leave town, tonight. I got some money saved, and..."

"You just don't get it. I can't leave. I owe to da dead to take revenge. I can't let my niggas death be in vain. I owe it to dem."

"But why? Pooh's dead. He ain't coming back. I loved my brother, and I think about him everyday. But what's done is done. You can't change the past, but we can look forward to our future."

"Lindsay, what da fuck you think I am…some all American dad living in da muthafuckin' country? Dis me, and dis what I'm about," he shouted, picking up a 9mm off the table, "and there ain't no fuckin' changin' me. Now leave!"

"No!" she firmly said, frowning at Squeeze. "I'm stayin' here with you. I'm pregnant with your child in me. Now you may think you can't change, but you can and you better. Look around you and look at your past. Everybody's dead or running from da law. You're the only one left from the crew, Squeeze. It could end here. You don't have to end up in the ground like Show or my brother. You have a choice," Lindsay pleaded, remembering her mother's words about Squeeze. Men like him don't last too long on this earth. They either end up in jail or in the grave.

"I love you, Squeeze," she continued, being in full tears. "And if I lose you like I lost my brother, I don't know what I'm gonna do. Please stop this gansta shit. Please Squeeze. I have a bad feeling. End this war before it's too late."

Squeeze stared at Lindsay with a bit of compassion. She stood butt-naked in front of him and confessed her love for him. Squeeze remembered that she was that little girl who he met back in the day with the long pigtails in her hair and hanging on to her older brother like he was her savior. He was amazed by how much she had grown, and how beautiful she had become. At first he had always looked at Lindsay like she was his little sister, but as months passed, he concealed his secret love for her. He never admitted it to her, but he loved Lindsay like he loved his wife. They had known each other forever.

Squeeze walked up to the weeping Lindsay and embraced her into his arms, and she warmly accepted by nestling her head against his chest, her tears trickling down her cheeks.

"Baby-doll, I'm gonna be all right. I promise you," Squeeze assured.

Hearing Squeeze call her baby-doll brought her some comfort. She loved his little nickname for her.

"This war will end, and after that, I promise everything will be like it was before," he continued, holding her still.

"Please don't leave me, Squeeze. Please. Promise me that," she said.

"I promise," he said. "I'm gonna handle everything soon."

He removed his arms from around her and said, "Baby-doll, I gotta go. You can stay if you want. I'll leave some men behind for your protection. You'll be okay, though."

With that, Lindsay grabbed her clothing to get dressed and watched Squeeze disappear out the door with a 9mm tucked in his waistband. She wasn't going anywhere. She was willing to stay, and wait for her man's safe return.

Bushwick, Brooklyn 11:20 p.m.

Promise sat crouched down low on the passenger side of his gray Nissan waiting for Trixie to exit out the brownstone on Gates Ave. For a young white woman, Trixie sure knew a lot of people in Brooklyn and had lots of resources. So far, he hadn't regretted bringing her along. Promise couldn't show his face around freely, so Trixie went into places and asked questions to her peoples she knew from her days when she used to turn tricks on Pennsylvania Ave.

She had started selling pussy when she was fourteen, and escaped from her abusive gorilla pimp at the age of seventeen. She fled to New Jersey and had stayed hidden from her pimp, Righteous, for over a year now. She was nervous being back in Brooklyn, but felt at home a little.

Waiting in the car for over a half-hour and trying to be inconspicuous, Promise held the loaded .45 in between his legs, being ready for anything. He continued to glance out the window, waiting for Trixie.

Trixie came strutting out of the building in some tight blue jeans, her brown leather coat, and some leather padlock shoes. She was smiling as she approached the car.

"What you got for me?" Promise asked.

"A lot," she replied, poppin' the gum in her mouth loudly, looking at Promise. "I told you I got you."

"And?"

"My peoples always lookin' out for me. But anyways, they say a lot's been goin' on, murder like crazy out here. My homeboy, Chaz, he knows some peoples in Bed-Stuy dat he do business with on a regular, and they say your boy is hiding out in some rundown liquor spot on Bedford. You owe me, Gene," she said. "I had to give him sump'n."

"I owe you."

"You lucky you're cute," she returned, poppin' the gum in her mouth again, and putting the car in drive and pulling off.

UPN-9 news, fox five news, Eyewitness news, and many more news stations were endlessly broadcasting the horrendous murders that had taken place in Harlem a few days ago. But what made the story widespread and front-page news was that the mutilated victim, Knocky's DNA had been linked back to the family's murder in Canarsie. Traces of his semen were found in the woman he had murdered and raped.

Two days after they found Knocky, they found his brother Kenny in a ditch near the Henry Hudson Parkway, shot once in his head.

The media ate it up. They wanted a story. They hounded detectives like Henry McGuinness for answers, and asked if there was some kind of turf war taken place between two gangs in the city. They wanted to know were there more men involved. Who were suspects, were there drugs involved, is it mafia related?

McGuinness, being frustrated tried ignoring the media. He already had the feds on his back, threatening to take over his case because the city had been inundated by these ghastly type murders over the past few months.

He went over evidence inch by inch and ran the names of both brothers through the computer and it came back that they had a healthy and long rap sheet. Both men were career criminals, being arrested from everything to possession of crack/cocaine, assault, to arm robbery and attempted murder.

The murder investigation for Squeeze's family had been put to rest, but McGuinness knew that there was much more going on behind the scenes, like why they had murdered that family and who had murdered the two brothers and what were the reasons.

He knew it took much more than asking questions around the way, running names through police computers and researching clues and evidence. He contacted his confidential informant that he had workin' the streets for him for over a year now. McGuinness needed help, and he was even willing to pay his C.I. McGuinness paged his C.I. and hoped that he'd call back real soon.

1:50 a.m. Washington Heights

Carlos and his men pulled up to an isolated block near Baker's field waiting for Tooks to show up. Miguel sat shotgun and Manny rested in the back seat with an Uzi lying beside him, peering out the window at the night. Carlos was quiet. He was thinking about what a mistake it had been to hire two fools like the Anderson brothers for a hit. They were good at killing, but foolish. And it cost him to pack up quickly and leave the bodega on 218th street.

Tooks had requested to see him earlier, and Carlos agreed. He knew you don't diss a man like Tooks by not agreeing to meet, especially after he had hung up on him previously.

All three men waited patiently in the black Cadillac. A few minutes later, bright headlights appeared from behind their car, blinding Carlos' view from his rearview. The black Dodge Ram pulled up close behind the Cadillac and stopped. Three men stepped out. Carlos and his men followed suit approaching Tooks and his men.

Carlos didn't recognize any of the men that Tooks had with him. Tooks had on a long leather trench coat with a blank look.

"I wanna talk to you in private," Tooks said, staring at

Carlos.

Carlos gave Tooks' men a quick glance and followed Tooks further away from his men and ear distant.

"What happened in Harlem?" Tooks asked. "Niggas got careless," Carlos replied. "I had to take care of it. I know that puta probably stalkin' my place on Broadway right now because of Knocky's big fuckin' mouth."

"You need to handle that. I need information, and I need it quickly," Tooks stated, referring to the whereabouts of Promise.

"You'll get your information, Tooks. I told you I'm gonna handle things," Carlos replied, holding Tooks' mean gaze. He respected Tooks, but wasn't intimidated by him.

"Handle them subtly, Carlos.... not like some wild hot-head cowboy. There's too much heat in the city from your ruthless ways."

"I do things my way Tooks. If you don't like it, too bad. I send a clear message."

"The feds are on me," Tooks explained.

"And...?" Carlos answered nonchalantly.

"This war needs to end quickly, before the feds start investigating, and once they get involved, Carlos, they won't stop until you and your crew are locked up for an ample amount of time."

Carlos looked unaffected by Tooks' warnings. "And when they come, or if they do come, dis is how I'm gonna handle it," Carlos said, lifting his shirt and revealing a 9mm tucked in his waistband.

"Young and foolish," Tooks replied with an irate look on his face. "A generation of fools."

Carlos sighed. "Whatever! What you got for me anyway?" Carlos asked, suddenly looking impatient.

Tooks looked over at his men and snapped his fingers. One of his brazen soldiers suddenly started to walk near Tooks and Carlos. He had a large package clutched in his hand. He walked up to Tooks and passed him the package, and walked off with no words being said.

Tooks passed Carlos the package. "Take it. It will come in handy."

"What da fuck is this?"

"Information."

"About what?" Carlos asked, inspecting the package.

Carlos began opening the package, and pulled out two glossy photos of two men, and typed information of a Brooklyn address next to the photos.

"His name his Nappy Head Don, and his partner, Rude Bwoy Rex, they run business out on Flatbush, just a few blocks from where your brother and cousin were killed. Word is these two men are the ones responsible for kidnapping and raping Tara. Two ruthless individuals. They're very connected to Squeeze. On that sheet are names and addresses of the two… complimentary of a Brooklyn precinct that owed me a favor," Tooks informed. "I trust you know what to do with the information."

Carlos nodded, staring at the photos and seething with rage thinking that these two men put their nasty hands on Tara and killed his woman, and had the audacity to leave her naked body in Prospect Park.

"I'm definitely gonna take care of it," Carlos said. "When I'm done wit' dem, dey gonna wish dey never heard of my name."

"Be subtle about it, Carlos."

"Fuck subtle, Tooks," he uttered, then started raving something in Spanish.

"All I want from you is information, Carlos," Tooks once again explained.

"I got you, Tooks," Carlos said, and made his way back over to his crew.

Tooks stood and watched the Cadillac pull off. He knew he could have taken care of the situation himself...but why get his hands dirty, especially when he knew Feds were investigating him again. He used Carlos as his pawn.

Bed-Stuy, BK, N.Y. 10:00 p.m.

Promise and Trixie sat parked across the street from Squeeze spot on Bedford.

"That's it?" Trixie asked.

"I guess so."

"So what are we waiting for, let's go see your boy. Shit you had us driving all around town tryin' to find information about him, and now you lookin' hesitant. Let's do this," Trixie said, looking eager.

"Chill fo' a minute," Promise replied with his eyes fixated on the rundown liquor store. He knew Squeeze, and he just didn't want to run up in there like everything was all good and shit. They weren't on the best of terms.

Promise was watching, and studying the spot. He noticed the surveillance camera outside. He noticed that there was an armed man inside the door whenever anyone went in or out. But the one thing that he saw that worked in his favor was they were ordering a lot of Chinese food from inside. Deliveries were coming like every two hours. Promise was going to try and use it to his advantage.

They watched the spot for hours, and Trixie was gettin' impatient. She continually popped the gum in her mouth, and nagged for Promise to do something. She even volunteered herself to knock on the front door and ask for the man herself.

"Ahight, this is what we gonna do. When we see the next delivery being dropped off, we make our move," he said.

"Bout time," she snapped back.

An hour later, the deliveryman pulled up to the location in his beat-up Honda Accord. Quickly, Promise and Trixie stepped out of the car, and walked across the street.

The Chinese man stepped out of his car with his phone glued to his ear. He was calling the location to confirm the delivery. Moments later, a slim thuggish lookin' male stepped outside to pick up the food. Promise watched the young thug pay the deliveryman and grabbed the food. But before he could step back inside, he was rushed by Promise with a .45 pressed against his temple.

"Nigga don't fuckin' move, or I'll blow your fuckin' head off," Promise threatened.

Trixie was right behind him, gripping a .45.

"Just chill, nigga," the thug casually replied, with his arms slightly to his side, with the food in the plastic carrier dangling from his grip. "We cool, right?"

"Move slowly," Promise ordered. "Dem cameras work?"

The thug nodded.

"Trixie, pat him down," Promise instructed.

She did, removing a loaded Glock from his waistband. Being covered by night, Promise gripped the thug by his arm, the cold steel pressed to the back of his head. Promise was ready for anything as he made his captive move slowly towards the door.

"How many inside?" Promise asked.

The thug looked reluctant to answer, until Promise gave him a quick and hard knock against the back of his head.

"About five," the thug answered, knowing he had seriously fucked up and wishing he could kill Promise.

"Ahight, dis is how it's gonna go down. I'm right behind you with dis gun pressed to da back of your head. Anything fucked up happens, and your brains will see daylight. You understand?"

The thug nodded.

Being careful not to be in the camera's view, Promise moved slowly to the entrance. He made his hostage knock on the door and scream out, "I got the food, let me in."

Without a reply, the door slowly opened, and with that, Promise pushed his captive in, with Trixie right behind him and had the element of surprise by springing into action, as him and Trixie quickly had everyone in awe while she held them at gunpoint.

"Nobody fuckin' move!" Promise yelled.

Trixie aimed her .45 aimlessly at whoever her eyes suddenly set on. She wasn't nervous, but new to the gun thing.

"What da fuck is this?" one of the men shouted.

"Squeeze, where da fuck is he?" Promise asked. This was his element. Being a stick-up kid for so many years, he definitely knew how to handle himself and play things out.

Still gripping his captive tightly by his arm he learned his name was Jah. Promise trained his gat on the two other men across the room who looked like they were willing to make a move against him.

"I swear, any funny business, and tomorrow ain't comin' for y'all," he warned.

The two suspicious men in the back slowly put their arms in the air with their eyes glued on Promise and remained still.

Promise made his way toward a back office, and found Squeeze sitting behind his desk, looking indifferent, as Promise stepped into the room with his gun in hand. Trixie followed.

"Promise, you're definitely a piece of work," Squeeze said. "How da fuck did you find me?"

"I got my ways, Squeeze," Promise replied, letting Jah go. "Remember we used to do this for a living."

"Who da fuck is da Barbie doll?" Squeeze asked.

"Trixie," she answered.

"Every time we meet, you around some new bitch," Squeeze stated.

"Boss, you okay?" one of Squeeze's men asked, walking into the office and glaring at Promise.

"Yeah, I got dis. I don't even know what I'm payin' y'all for, if y'all can't even keep dis asshole out," Squeeze chided.

Squeeze henchmen looked fiercely at Promise and slowly backed out the room.

"What da fuck you want, Promise? Dis ain't back in da

day no more… a lot of shit done changed between us," Squeeze proclaimed.

"I understand, but I need your help," Promise said.

"Help? Nigga what makes you think I wanna help you, after you done robbed me and Show? And now you run up in here wit' guns out, like it's love like dat."

"Cuz, in return, I got your back, like how we used to be back in da day. I'm sorry about what happened to your family, Squeeze. But together, we can make it right. Right now Squeeze, I ain't got nuthin' to lose, and wit' dis war you got goin' wit' these Dominicans, you gonna need all the help and soldiers you need on your side."

"And in return, what do you want from me?" Squeeze asked, reclining back in his La-Z boy leather chair and staring at Promise.

"I want my daughter back in my life."

"And how am I supposed to make dat happen?"

"You got resources and money…I know you can track her down for me…see where she's located. I just need information about her whereabouts," Promise said.

"What if I can't?"

"I know you can," Promise replied. "I got your back on dis war, Squeeze. This is all I want from you. You owe me dis, Squeeze. Because of you, she was taken away from me in da first place."

"Nigga, you da one dat shot da cop," Squeeze reminded him.

"Cuz I had your back dat night," Promise countered. "Now I need you to have my back on this."

Squeeze was quiet, staring at Promise. At first he looked reluctant.

"Ahight, we got a deal. But Promise, if you cross me..."

"I won't," he assured.

Squeeze stood up and walked over to Promise. A faint smile appeared on Squeeze face. He gave Promise dap and embraced him into a manly hug. "Despite everything, it's good to see you again, my nigga," Squeeze stated.

"Same here, Squeeze...let bygones be bygones?"

"Man, dat shit is water under da bridge," Squeeze replied.

Promise felt a bit comfortable. "We da only ones left from da crew. I got your back; you have my word on that, Squeeze."

Squeeze nodded and returned with, "Same here, Promise. Together, we end dis shit."

And with that, the two reconciled their differences, and were ready for anything. Moments later, Promise was surprised to see Lindsay walk into the room. He stared at her incredulously, and then glanced at Squeeze.

"Promise?" Lindsay asked in disbelief. "Ohmigod!"

"Lindsay, oh shit...say word," Promise replied.

Lindsay ran up to him and gave him a lovin' hug. "I'm so happy to see that you're okay," she stated.

Trixie stood off to the side, frowning at Lindsay. Even though Promise wasn't her man, and she only knew him for almost two weeks, she felt connected like Bonnie and Clyde. She felt helpless as she watched this beautiful black woman hug up on the man she had a crush on.

Lindsay turned her attention to Trixie and asked, "Who's

your friend?"

"Lindsay, Trixie…Trixie, Lindsay," he introduced.

"Hey, nice to meet you," Lindsay greeted by smiling and extended her hand.

"Whateva. Likewise," Trixie sarcastically returned with attitude.

"Okay, he's only a friend sweetheart, nothing else," Lindsay said stepping away from Trixie.

Trixie sighed and moved in closer to Promise. He and Lindsay talked and caught up on lost time. But Lindsay became nervous knowing that Promise's arrival wasn't a good thing for her, knowing that he and Squeeze were definitely up to something no good. She was excited to see a friend again, but at the same time knowing he was on the run for murdering a cop made her very nervous.

Letting old friends be, she went into the back room and called up her mother to inform her about her location. She knew her moms would be worrying sick about her.

When her mother answered, Lindsay cried out, "Mother, please pray for me."

11:00 p.m. Canarsie Pier, Brooklyn.

Detective McGuiness drove onto Canarsie pier slowly, looking for his informant. Being that it was cold and soon to be winter the parking lot was sparse with cars and people, with a full moon casting over the pier.

McGuiness spotted his informant at the lower end of the pier, leaning over the guardrail peering out at the ocean. He pulled his red Dodge Caravan into a parking spot and quickly stepped out. The wind from the sea slightly nipped at his skin as he approached his C.I. He zipped up his leather bomber, and pulled out a cigarette from his coat.

He moved toward his C.I. in silence and stood a few feet away from him, and looked straight ahead into the ocean as he leaned forward over and against the railing and placed the unlit cigarette between his lips.

Without even turning to face his informant, McGuiness continued to peer out into the ocean and asked, "So, what you got for me?"

"Damn, not even a hello, how you're doin', just straight to da point, huh?" His informant replied, glancing at McGuiness.

Looking like a hustler, he was dressed in dark clothing, a black hoodie, a clean leather coat, black timberlands, and a bulky long costly chain dangled from around his neck.

He felt it was safe to meet McGuiness out in Brooklyn over by the pier. No one knew him there as they did in Washington Heights. McGuiness' informant massaged his goatee and said, "I'm only doin' dis cause this shit needs to stop, McGuiness. This war that Carlos got us in, got too much heat on everybody. Niggas can't even eat any more cuz cops harassing us like crazy, and dey talkin' about involvin' da feds."

"This city is going to shit anyway," McGuiness uttered, glancing at his C.I. "You got a light?"

His C.I. reached into his coat pocket and pulled out a lighter, sparking up McGuiness' Newport. McGuiness took a long drag and slowly exhaled a cloud of smoke from his mouth. "Thanks."

Both men gazed out into the ocean for a moment, before McGuiness spoke up and said, "Ahight, I ain't come out here for the view, talk to me, Manny."

"Shit is about to really go down, McGuiness. Carlos lost it. He don't give a fuck anymore. It's strictly about revenge wit' him," Manny explained.

"What can you give me?"

"Everything, from the club shooting that happened at the Brooklyn Café a few months ago, to that family that was murdered out here a few weeks back."

McGuiness nodded. "Are you willing to testify to the grand jury about this?"

Manny appeared hesitant.

"Manny, I need you in this case, without you, I ain't got shit," McGuiness pushed.

"Can I get full amnesty if I do?" he asked.

"I can't promise you that. That's only up to the D.A. and a Judge."

"McGuiness, I got twins about to be born. My girl is six months pregnant."

"Congratulations."

"This is da only reason why I'm doin' this," Manny continued. "My ol' lady stressin' me hard. She keeps having these dreams about me dying. And it's scarin' da shit out of me, to be honest. I don't wanna die or go to jail without even gettin' to know my babies."

"The best I can do for you is tell the Judge and D.A. how well you cooperated. But they gonna want some solid evidence and information on Carlos and his crew."

"What if I told you about a hit that's suppose to go down soon in Brooklyn?"

"Keep talking."

"Carlos got sudden information on the men responsible for Tara's murder and rape. Some Rasta's or Jamaicans, whateva the fuck they call themselves are located somewhere on Flatbush Ave. He strappin' to go handle his business wit' a crew of armed men as we speak. They about to turn Brooklyn into a fuckin' bloodbath, McGuiness," Manny informed.

"Do you know exactly when this hit is gonna take place?" McGuiness asked.

"Nah, he ain't give the word out yet. But it's definitely coming."

"What about names. Who is he going after?"

"All I can give you is some hot-shot Jamaican from Brooklyn who goes by da name Nappy head Don."

"Manny, listen...I want you to keep in touch with me on day by day basis. You hear me? The minute you hear when and where it's going down, you call me," McGuiness insisted, being up in Manny's face.

"Yeah, I got you."

"This war has got to end," McGuiness said.

Manny looked at McGuiness as he took another pull from

his cigarette and then tossed it into the ocean. Manny's gaze had a look of concern. "McGuiness, if I do testify...how it's gonna play out? I did a lot of dirt wit' Carlos, even played my hand in murder. I ain't a fuckin' saint. I don't want da Judge to look at me, and give me twenty-five to life. I can't do dat many years in prison."

"Sometimes, with this system, we're willing to deal with a lesser evil to fry the main fish. You willing to give up Carlos and help stop this bloodshed will have a considerate influence on the D.A. Just be honest with me, Manny. That's all I ask from you," McGuiness stated.

"I'm telling you everything dat I know."

They continued to talk and Manny broke down everything to McGuiness on how the war started, even bringing up the incident with Pooh, and Manny was also involved in Pooh's death, too. His loose lips ran freely for forty minutes.

As McGuiness was about to walk away from their discreet meeting, the cold air from the ocean finally taking it's affect on him, he slightly tapped Manny on his shoulder and said, "Watch your back out there, Manny."

Manny nodded and continued to peer out into the ocean. He was scared, but felt that this had to be done. He wanted to see his children born, and he knew that if he kept fuckin' around with Carlos, he'd probably never see his twins breathe their first breaths. He was having a change of heart about everything he did in his life.

8:50 p.m. Washington Heights

"Manny, where you been? We've been callin' you since last night," Miguel asked, staring at Manny. "It's about to go down."

"What?" Manny replied looking aloof.

"It's on. You down for some 187 tonight?" Miguel asked, shoving a full clip into a .45.

"Whatever, yo."

"Carlos got wind on their location of dem two dreads on Flatbush. We gonna take care of business tonight. We rollin' deep out there and gonna fuck these niggas up, Manny. "

Manny had never been more nervous. He knew he couldn't back out; it would look suspicious on his part. He had been in many situations with his crew before, and always handling his business on the streets, but something about tonight had him wary. His pregnant girlfriend kept having horrible dreams about him dying, and that really bothered him.

Miguel passed Manny a loaded Uzi machine gun. Manny gripped the deadly weapon in his hand and thought about detective McGuinness. He needed to call him right away.

Manny let a few minutes pass before he was able to slip away unnoticed and pull out his cell phone to call McGuinness. He had to watch his surroundings carefully, because if Carlos and the rest found out that he was a snitch, he wouldn't make it past the doorway alive.

He dialed McGuinness and successfully informed him about how the hits were going down tonight. Half-hour later, two truckloads of gung ho Dominicans raced to Brooklyn.

10:35 p.m. Brooklyn N.Y.

On the corner of Church and Flatbush Avenues, on a cold and calm night, Nappy Head Don and his men lingered around luxurious parked cars, drinking, smokin' Dro, and discussing business. All five men had fierce reputations in the hood, and intimidated residents by their thuggish demeanors and wild ways.

Nappy Head Don stood next to his most feared enforcer, Rude Bwoy Rex, with his dreads tied tightly together in a few rubber bands, and adorning a broad black Sean John coat, concealing a Glock 17 under his coat, and gripping an open bottle of Wray and Nephew Jamaican rum in his hand. But his boy, Rude Bwoy Rex had a nickel-plated stainless steel barrel shotgun hidden underneath his bulky winter coat. Rude Bwoy Rex was always ready for anything. In his line of business, he knew he had made too many enemies on the streets to get caught out there without a weapon.

"Tooks, what mi tell yuh bout comin up short wi' mi cash... spit blood-fire wit' dis shit here," Nappy head Don scolded one of his workers.

"I'm sorry Nappy, but cops out here are on some crazy shit…I can't get shit done right without 5-0 always on my back," Tooks casually responded, staring Nappy head Don square in his eyes, knowing he respected eye contact since he felt if he looked in your eyes he could tell if you was lying.

"Yuh think' mi give a fuck about police, fuck dem batty

boys...mi want yuh to come correct next time, or don't come at all...yuh hear, bredren?"

Tooks nodded, and replied, "Yeah, I hear you Nappy." Tooks then glanced at Rude Bwoy Rex, and smirked at him. He made Tooks really nervous, as he stared into the eyes of cold-blooded killer.

Tooks walked away, being intimidated by Nappy Head Don, Rude Bwoy Rex, and his men, as they loitered around on the corner drinking and taking pulls from the burning Dro.

Nappy Head Don continued to talk quietly with Rude Bwoy Rex, and taking sips of the Jamaican Rum to keep him warm from the cold. Both men had pussy on their minds, as they talked about Mary and Tay, two chicken-head females from around the way who were down for anything when it came to Nappy Head Don and Rude Bwoy Rex.

Rude Bwoy Rex smiled, which was very rare, when he thought about pushing his nine and a half snake dick into Mary tonight. Nappy Head Don stared at his friend and partner in crime, and smiled too, thinking the same thing.

Wasting no time, Nappy Head Don got on the phone and called Tay to inform them that they were coming over soon.

Parked half a block down from Church on Flatbush, Carlos stared at Nappy Head Don and Rude Bwoy Rex with rage, seething with revenge. An Uzi rested on his lap, as he sat shotgun in the H2 Hummer.

Miguel was the driver, and Manny and another soldier were seated in the back seat. Behind them was another H2 filled with men who were in a killing mood.

Manny sat impatiently, hoping that his call with detective McGuiness was a success. He gripped a 9mm in his hand and stared down the block at the Jamaicans who were gathered around in the cold. He killed before, but tonight he finally had a conscience. And he prayed that some kind of miracle would intervene between tonight's actions.

"How you wanna do dis?" Miguel asked.

"Just drive," Carlos dryly responded.

"Yo, Carlos, we need to think about dis for a minute," Manny interjected, stalling for time.

"Nigga, think about what?" Carlos chided back. "Putas killed Tara, killed my brother, my cousin, and tonight, I'm gonna kill them. Miguel, drive!" he shouted.

"But, Carlos…" Manny began to say.

"Manny shut da fuck up! Or I'll leave you dead in Brooklyn with them Jamaicans."

Manny let out a dreadful sigh and kept his mouth shut.

Obeying orders, Miguel put the H2 in drive, left the headlights off, and slowly began cruising down Flatbush, with the second H2 following. Guns were cocked back, loaded, and ready for murder and death.

Nappy Head Don was still on the phone talking to Tay trying to arrange to get himself some pussy for the night. Rude Bwoy Rex was leaning against his CLK 350 coupe, listening to his man set up some sex for the night and watching the crew roll dice and exchange money in the cold. He took a pull from the burning Dro, and glanced to his right and suddenly noticed a black Hummer approaching them with its headlights off. He became suspicious and gripped his shotgun underneath his coat.

Nappy Head Don turned with the phone still pressed to his ear, noticing the truck coming towards them, and shouted, "Blood clat, fuck! It's a hit!"

He dropped the phone and clutched his Glock. Rude Bwoy Rex pulled out his shotgun and began firing away at the H2, shattering the windshield and blowing away Miguel from inside, causing him to slump over the staring wheel dead.

Carlos quickly exited the truck and his Uzi exploded into the night, quickly mowing down two of Nappy Head Don's men. Manny ran out and shot at Rude Bwoy Rex, becoming furious after seeing his man, Miguel, blown away.

Rude Bwoy Rex didn't let up with the shotgun, as he hammered off round after round at Carlos and his men.

The second H2 came with serious back up, as all three men gripped an Uzi and let off a hail of gunfire at the Jamaicans.

"Blood-claat...fuck yuh..." Nappy Head Don screamed, shooting round after round at his enemies, as he took cover behind

Rude Bwoy Rex's coupe.

Rude Bwoy Rex walked into the line of fire, pulling out his Glock 18 and instantly killing two Dominicans that came his way.

Bam. Bam. Bam. Bam. Bam. Bam. He continued firing, glaring at Manny, who was reloading. Rude Bwoy Rex aimed the Glock at Manny and shot him twice, laying him out on the cold concrete. But soon afterwards, the slugs of an Uzi exploding from Carlos' hands cut down Rude Bwoy Rex.

Nappy Head Don stared at his boy Rude Bwoy Rex sprawled out on the street.

"Yuh blood-claat batty boy…mi come fi yuh…yuh hear… yuh gun down mi friend…mi fuckin' kill yuh!" Nappy Head Don screamed.

Police sirens abruptly pierced the air, they were coming deep and they were coming fast. With the few men he had left, Carlos retreated in the second H2 and drove hastily down Flatbush. But Nappy Head Don wasn't so lucky, cops quickly surrounded him as he tried to flee in Rude Bwoy Rex's coupe.

"Get out the car now!" a uniformed officer screamed, pointing his weapon at the driver's side window.

"Driver, drop the weapon and get out the car! Now!"

Over a dozen officers were on the scene, and every cop had their gun out and aimed at Nappy Head Don.

Still seated behind the steering wheel, bleeding and outnumbered, Nappy Head Don contemplated his fate. His Glock 17 was still gripped in his hand, and he peered out the window and saw his right hand man who he had known all of his life, sprawled out on the street.

"Mi ain't scared of police…fuck y'all. Fuck da bate boy

blood-claat cops," Nappy Head Don screamed.

"Driver, drop the gun out the window and exit the car slowly!"

Nappy Head Don's face was twisted with rage and anger. He wasn't going to prison. Or worst, get deported back to Jamaica cause he was in the U.S. illegally. He had a huge bounty on his head in Jamaica.

The standoff went on for about fifteen minutes, and shortly the media was on hand covering the confrontation live for all of New York to see. Knowing that he was at a dead end, Nappy Head Don finally made up his mind after deciding what he had to do.

Shockingly, he fired three shots out the passenger side window, striking a female cop in her gut. He quickly exited the vehicle blasting away, and was able to shoot another uniform officer in his chest before he was gunned down in a barrage of bullets by the police. He took over two-dozen rounds into his body and dropped on the ground, dead. And it was all caught on film.

McGuiness briskly walked down the corridor of Kings County hospital looking for a patient. He heard that Manny was still alive and needed to talk to him, if he was able to talk.

He deeply regretted that his police department didn't get to the scene on time to stop the bloodshed and carnage that happened 24 hours ago leaving six men dead, one cop dead, and another cop critically wounded. He had pleaded with the captain and a few others to put out arrest warrants, surveillance on the location that Manny had given him, and enough man power to arrest the culprits. But his captain denied his request for everything, because he wasn't too sure of how credible McGuiness' C.I. was.

Everything was boiling over. The carnage in Brooklyn made front-page news for days, was aired on every news station and channel from New York to L.A., and caused chaos in the NYPD. The mayor made an announcement on television proclaiming his condolences for the slain officer on duty, and the one in critical condition at Kings County hospital. He promised that the men responsible who were still on the loose would be caught, tried, and justice would be done. His words were harsh and assuring.

The feds officially took over the cases and stormed into the NYPD precincts in Brooklyn and Washington Heights like wildfire demanding records, information and cases be handed over to them. They wanted everything that they had on Carlos, and Squeeze, and anyone else involved because this war was out of control and causing havoc on the city.

McGuiness strolled up to room 328, and peered at Manny lying still in bed with tubes running in and out of him, and he noticed that he was handcuffed to the bed railing. McGuiness sighed deeply and felt guilty that he wasn't able to help Manny in time. There was a cop posted outside his hospital room, and McGuiness spoke to him briefly.

Soon the nurse walked into Manny's room and checked his vitals. McGuiness stopped her before she was able to exit and asked, "How is he holding up? What's his condition?"

The nurse gave him a grave look and somberly replied

with, "I'm sorry to say, but he may never walk again. The bullet struck near his spinal cord, shifting it severely, and we weren't able to retrieve the bullet from out his back. I'm sorry."

"Thank you," he said, and watched the nurse leave the room.

McGuiness peered at Manny, who looked barely awake. He felt sorry for Manny. He became angry and frustrated with himself and the NYPD for taking his inside tip so lightly. Now Manny was a cripple, after he had come and asked for his help. McGuiness made up his mind that he was going to retire and receive his full pension after twenty-five years on the force. But before that happened, he was going to do one more thing to make sure Manny's incident didn't go unnoticed.

He said a quick prayer over Manny's bedside and wished him the best. Afterwards, he left the hospital, took out his cell phone and called up a reporter he knew from The Daily News and ran down all the information to his friend reporter about what he knew, how the war was started, the key players involved, the NYPD's lack of information on certain people, and also how the NYPD didn't't' immediately respond to an inside tip he had received from his C.I. Then he explained how last night's bloodshed could have been prevented.

It was McGuiness' way of saying fuck the NYPD!

6:15 p.m. Garrison, New York.

Tooks sat back in the plush passenger seat of Johnny's sleek black Escalade, enduring the hour long ride upstate, and thinking about the chaos Carlos had caused in Brooklyn. It was all over town, as the feds and ATF were knocking down doors all over the city making ample arrests, and indicting key players all over New York. Tooks wasn't surprised that former Gambino soldier and associate Dante "Fetch" Leotardo requested to meet with Tooks instantaneously in his stylish and grand upstate home.

Johnny navigated the SUV through the winding, dimly lit roads of Garrison N.Y. Both men were quiet, not even the radio was playing. Tooks peered out the passenger side window, gazing at the masses of trees that flew by as the truck zipped by the dense woods doing 65, with dusk settling overhead. Tooks heard the calm hum of the engine moving up the hills as they came closer to their destination.

Johnny glanced at his friend, Tooks, and knew he was stressed with worries. He wanted to say something to ease his friend's tension, but decided against it, and continued to focus his attention on the road.

Soon after, the Escalade came across an impressive and classy gated contemporary home that was nestled in the lush greenery of the Hudson River valley and further protected by a contiguous 25-acre land preserve.

The truck stopped at a 10-foot Iron Gate, with two armed men standing guard out front.

Johnny rolled down the driver's side window and stated,

"Mr. Dante Leotardo requested our presences tonight."

The beefy guard radioed the attendant of the house and moments later, Tooks and Johnny were confirmed. The armed guard signaled for the gate to be opened, and Johnny slowly moved his truck inside the estate and climbed up the gravel hill.

They stopped in front of a grand 12-room home with two large pillars out front, and a picturesque view of the land downhill.

Tooks stepped out the Escalade and walked toward the home. Outside the entrance was a male servant in a tuxedo waiting for their arrival.

"Mr. Leotardo requests your presence in the great room," the servant said, motioning with his hand for the guests to come in.

Tooks walked in, followed by Johnny. The servant then led them back to the huge great room decorated and furnished mostly with an antique feel of the early 20th century. Above their heads was an enormous skylight. Tooks and Johnny stood in the room unaffected by the stylish home.

Moments later, Mr. Dante "Fetch" Leotardo stepped into the room draped in a long 100% cotton white Terry Velour robe, house slippers, and clutching a long stemmed glass filled with red wine. A beautiful brunette who had long hair, a thin waistline, long legs, and a bubbly personality flanked him. The same robe adorned her. It seemed that both of them had just came out of the sauna or pool.

"Gentlemen, please have a seat," Mr. Leotardo gestured with his hand. He was five feet, eight, thin, with salt and peppered hair, having crows feet at the edge of his eyes, clean shaven, and had a menacing stare that intimidated anyone who he met.

Dante Leotardo killed many men, and murdered his way to the top, gaining the respect of the streets and his associates. But that was many years ago, and he was now a calmer business minded man in his early fifties.

"All due respect, but I would rather stand, Mr. Leotardo," Tooks said, holding Leotardo's gaze.

"Fine with me."

Leotardo turned to his beautiful mistress and said, "Honey, give us a minute to discuss business. I'll be around shortly."

"Okay, D.L," she replied, smiling and giving him a quick kiss on the lips.

Then she turned and glanced at Tooks who she thought was a very attractive black male, standing tall in a leather jacket and short dark black hair. Tooks noticed the twinkle in her eyes and remained impassive. The beautiful brunette exited the room leaving the three gentlemen to discuss business.

Soon as his mistress was out the room, he turned to Tooks and calmly, but sternly asked, "What the fuck is going on with the niggers and spics in that city Tooks? I'm getting calls from my men downtown and in Brooklyn stating that the cops are busting their balls because of a war. Now usually, I don't mind if niggers and spics kill each other, but when it starts to interfere with my business. I get upset."

"I understand," Tooks casually replied.

"Those are your people Tooks, that's your area, and I want you to handle that. I'm losing thousands of dollars a day, because some nigger decided to go gung ho. And some spic who thinks he's the next Tony Montana wants to prove a point."

Leotardo walked to the colossal size window casting a picturesque view of his downhill landscape, and sipped on his wine. With his back turned to Tooks and Johnny he continued with, "Now you wanted to retire, and I set you up with that BMW car dealership in Long Island. I gave you work when you was nothing but this petty, penniless, starving nigger trying to survive in Harlem. With my help, Tooks, you became a king over your people quickly. I supplied you. I supported you. You lived pretty good off of me, Tooks. Sometimes I look at you and think you're living too good."

Leotardo turned to face Tooks, and continued with, "And now you owe me, and I want this problem in the city handled quickly. And if you can't handle it, then believe me, I'll find some men that will."

In his world, and for health reasons, Tooks knew what Leotardo meant by that statement.

"I'll take care of it right away, Mr. Leotardo. You have my word on it," Tooks stated.

"I believe you. You never let me down before, Tooks. Please don't start now. We're both too old," Leotardo said. "By the end of the week, I want everything quiet in the city. I don't want to hear about any more bloodshed between that spic Carlos and him clashing with that nigger. Carlos is a fuckin' hothead anyway. I never liked that boy. Take care of it."

Tooks nodded, knowing what Leotardo was referring to. "I will."

He had to eat his pride when it came to Dante "Fetch" Leotardo constantly using the nigger word. Leotardo was from the old school where the word nigger was a common word back then implying to African Americans. And Tooks knew that without Leotardo he wouldn't be where he was today.

"Y'all may go," Leotardo said, waving them off. He watched them leave and then called his mistress back into the room.

Outside Leotardo's residence, Tooks confided with Johnny about his situation.

"I can't take Carlos out now, he's too valuable," Tooks explained.

"Why is that?" Johnny asked, looking at Tooks with a bewildered look.

"He's a pawn right now for me to get at a bigger prize," Tooks stated.

"But if you don't take out Carlos, Leotardo is not gonna be too happy, Tooks. He wants this war to end. It's fuckin' with everybody."

"Johnny, I want you to make a phone call out to your connections in Brooklyn. Tell them that I'm willing to put up twenty-five thousand dollars for any information that can link me up to Squeeze. Make sure to tell whoever bites, that I just want to talk to the man, and I don't mean any harm to him. Make it clear that I just want to talk. Tell whoever, that I have some information that he might want to hear."

"You sure about this, Tooks?"

"Make the phone call."

"I will."

Tooks knew it would come to this and he had to spread his wealth to get something done right. He needed to meet with Squeeze ASAP.

Brooklyn N.Y.

Squeeze sat at his desk pondering about Nappy head Don's sudden demise. He had heard it over the news and the streets were talking. He couldn't believe that Carlos got to Nappy so suddenly. It had him a bit worried, because he knew someone had leaked information out about Nappy's whereabouts.

The room was dark and quiet. He ordered his men to stay out of sight. He wanted to be alone. He knew an end was coming, because something just didn't feel right within him. He didn't know if it was Lindsay's talk about getting out of the game and having a family together, or having Promise around when he knew that he was a wanted man by the feds.

Promise kept good on his word and been by Squeeze's side since his arrival. But he knew having Promise around was too risky.

Squeeze got on his radio and instructed one of his men to have Promise come into his office.

Lindsay walked into the dim room to comfort her man.

"Baby, you okay?" she asked, walking up to him and resting down on his lap and throwing her arms around him, nestling next to him.

"Just thinkin'," Squeeze said, not even looking at her.

Fifteen minutes later, Promise walked into the room and Trixie was right behind him like she was attached to his hip.

"You call for me, Squeeze?" Promise asked, standing dead center of the room and staring at Squeeze.

Squeeze reached into his drawer and pulled out a small

white envelope and tossed it on his desk.

"That's for you," Squeeze mentioned.

"What is it?"

"Your daughter," he uttered.

Promise looked baffled. "What you mean?"

"That's the information you requested about your daughter's whereabouts, well there it is." He pointed to the envelope sitting on his desk. "I found her for you."

Promise looked speechless. He glanced back at Trixie and she shrugged.

"You serious?" Promise asked.

"She's in Camden, New Jersey, twenty minutes from Philly. She's in foster care with a couple named the Petersons. She's been there for six months now," Squeeze stated.

"How do you know all of this?" Promise asked.

"I got a girl that works for social services. She ran your daughter's name through the computer and hooked me up for a small fee of course. I owe it to you."

Promise walked up to the envelope and picked it up. He couldn't believe that he was so close to reuniting with his daughter. He was nervous.

"Leave and handle your business, nigga. And don't come back," Squeeze said.

"I don't know what to say, Squeeze…thank you. I owe you."

"Nah…fuck it, despite what happened between us…we still peoples. But don't come back around here anymore…get da fuck from here and never come back. Ain't no more memories here for us, Promise."

Promise nodded, understanding what Squeeze was saying.

"You take your daughter and try to get a better life for yourself," Squeeze added.

Squeeze got up and approached Promise, giving him dap and embracing him into a manly hug.

Lindsay stood behind Squeeze and couldn't wait to give Promise a hug. When they both let go, Lindsay went up to Promise and hugged him tightly. "Please be safe, Promise. I know I still have a brother left with you," she proclaimed. "You take your daughter and try and start over. Please."

After the moment, Promise and Trixie left the undisclosed liquor store on Bedford Avenue in the night and made their destination for Camden, New Jersey. Promise knew that after tonight, he would never see New York again.

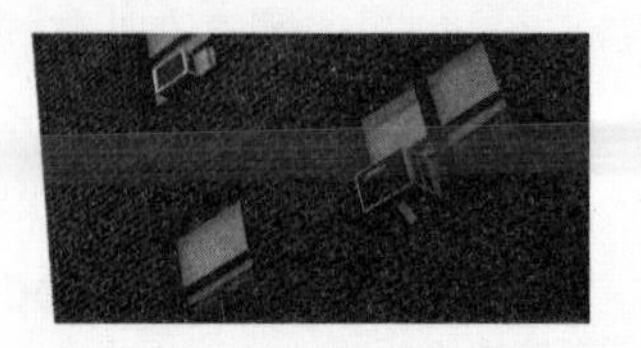

"Twenty-five thousand right, just to talk?" Knuckles asked Tooks, sitting in Johnny's Escalade that was parked on Jay Street in downtown Brooklyn. Knuckles bit and was still chewing.

"Yes. Tell your man that I wanna have a sit down with him," Tooks casually explained. "I want to exchange a bit of information with him."

"You got the money on you right now?" Knuckles asked, eager for his payday.

Tooks pulled out a bulky envelope from his coat and

passed it to Knuckles who was in the backseat. Knuckles grabbed the envelope, opened it, and flipped through C-notes, smiling.

"We have an agreement?" Tooks asked.

"Yeah, we cool."

Knuckles got on his cell phone and called Squeeze immediately. He began explaining to Squeeze about how Tooks wanted to meet with him right away and share important information. Squeeze was reluctant at first, thinking it had to be a set up. He didn't trust it. But then he changed his mind and agreed to the meeting; the only stipulation was that Tooks had to meet with Squeeze wearing a blindfold at Squeeze's spot.

It was too risky at first for Tooks and Johnny, but Tooks agreed, trusting his instincts. Squeeze sent a handful of men out to Tooks' destination and picked him and Johnny up in a truck.

Half-hour later the truck pulled up to the back entrance of the location, and two men grabbed Tooks and Johnny by their arms and led them inside.

They led Tooks and Johnny to Squeeze's back office and made them have a seat. Then they took the blindfolds off. Six men stood around in the room, glaring at Tooks and his friend. Squeeze was seated behind his desk, gazing at Tooks, finally meeting the notorious Tooks. Squeeze wasn't impressed. To him, Tooks looked like some average fifty-year old man that was dressed sharply in a gray suit and a long leather trench coat. Squeeze thought that Tooks would look like a menacing looking man with scars running across his face.

"First off, let me set it straight when I say that Harlem shit doesn't fly in Bed-Stuy," Squeeze proclaimed.

"I'm only here on business," Tooks smoothly replied,

holding Squeeze's gaze.

He and Johnny were relaxed and acted like they were among friends. They were unarmed and still held a strong presence.

"What you want from me?" Squeeze asked, getting to the point.

"Information," Tooks replied. "You have something that I want, and I have something that you want."

"Before dis goes on, I have one question," Squeeze blurted.

"Go on."

"Did you have a hand in murdering my family?" Squeeze asked, suspecting if he did, he probably wouldn't be honest about it in the first place.

"You have my word. I was not responsible for that. But I can give you the man who was," Tooks stated.

"I'm listening," Squeeze said, reclining back in his leather chair.

"You and I both know that this war between you and him can't go on any longer. It's bringing too much heat on everyone, and my associates are losing tons of money everyday. The feds are involved, police are constantly knocking in doors, and the mayor is calling y'all a terrorist threat to his city. Things need to calm down and calm down fast. Now I have a proposal to make that happen."

"Like what?"

"I'll give you Carlos. I have his location. He's weak. He lost two of his best men in that shootout with the Jamaicans."

"And for what in return?" Squeeze asked.

Tooks glanced at Johnny and then looked at Squeeze and said, "I'll give you Carlos in return for Promise."

"Promise?" Squeeze said, looking confused. "Fuck you want wit' him?"

"Let's just say, it's personal."

"How personal?"

"I don't care to disclose details at this moment. But you give me information on your boy; I'll give you Carlos, and his business and corners in Washington Heights. And you have my word; you can run his operation with no interference from my peoples or any other organization around that area."

"That's a sweet deal, Squeeze," Knuckles chimed in, glancing at his boy.

Squeeze looked hesitant. Promise had left two days ago to get his daughter. And they had grown up together. But he wanted Carlos so bad his dick was hard. He was in a tight spot.

Squeeze clasped his hands together and started thinking. He looked at Tooks and asked, "You sure your information is accurate?"

"I should be asking the same thing about you," Tooks countered. "Carlos depends on me. He came to me for help. This is your one opportunity to end this for good."

"Squeeze, you don't owe Promise nuthin," Knuckles persuaded. "This is about the future now. Da past belongs in da past...and we need to handle our business. That nigga murdered your family, nigga get yours."

Squeeze sighed and reluctantly said, "Ahight, nigga…we have a deal."

Moments later, Tooks and Johnny were escorted back

outside and into the parked truck. Tooks was a happy man, now knowing where Promise was heading to find his daughter. He planned to greet him personally.

Lindsay remained distant in the backdrop, noticing something big had gone down. When she saw Tooks and Johnny leave the building, she knew Squeeze was up to no good, and wanted to know what was going on.

When she tried to confront Squeeze, he quickly shut her out, exclaiming to her that he was gonna finally take care of his business. She saw many guns and knives displayed everywhere, with cutthroat men loading rounds and clips into Uzi's and machine guns, and her heart became troubled.

"Squeeze, I know what you're up too… please, just let it be. You don't have to go after him!" she shouted.

"Bitch, you crazy!" Squeeze shouted back. "Dat nigga murdered my family. He gonna get his."

"No! I won't let you!" she exclaimed, running up to Squeeze and grabbing him tightly by his shirt. "Think about us, and your baby that I'm carrying. Please!"

"Get da fuck off me, Lindsay! Dis ain't about you anymore! Now get off me!"

"No! I'm not letting you go!"

"Yo, get dis bitch off of me," he commanded one of his men.

Knuckles went up to Lindsay, grabbed her tightly and began pulling at her.

"No! No! No! Y'all gonna get him killed," she cried out, still trying to hold onto Squeeze. But Knuckles and another soldier were persistent and pulled the howling Lindsay away from Squeeze and dragged her out the room and locked her out.

"No-o-o-o! Please, Squeeze. Don't do this."

She banged and kicked on the door, but the men inside completely ignored her. In a desperate attempt to stop Squeeze from causing more bloodshed and probably getting himself killed, Lindsay ran out of the building with her cell phone pressed to her ear and dialed.

"911 emergency," the operator said.

"Please, my boyfriend is going crazy. He's about to kill some people," Lindsay shouted frantically, tears trickling down her cheeks. "You need to stop him."

"Please give us your name and location."

"My name is Lindsay, and I'm at…"

tapped Trixie and silently mouthed, "Kick it to him."

Trixie smiled and then she reached for a piece of paper and a pen and wrote down her number.

"Here, I want you to have this." Trixie said as she handed the white man her phone number.

"What's this?" he asked.

"I want you to have that, and call me during the week and I'll make sure that I really thank you for this," Trixie said in a seductive tone.

The white man looked like a nerd but he caught on really quick as he began to turn bloodshot red from embarrassment.

Trixie then walked off with him and left me at the computer. As I sat there I remember feeling nervous with anticipation because I could sense that I just might possibly be reunited with my daughter. And the simple thought of just possibly seeing her was way too much for a nigga's blood pressure to handle.

Trixie soon made her way back to the computer and she had a wide smile on her face.

"What da fuck's so funny?" I asked.

"Nothing. It's just that I could have got that dude for like $250 for a blowjob. I know I could have!" Trixie confidently stated.

"Trixie you got more game than a state fair. Fo' real fo' real!"

"Yeah but we gotta get this info. I'm gonna print it out and then we should be good. We just gotta hope that Ashley is at one of these addresses," Trixe explained.

When we were done printing the info I was more than ready to get the hell up outta that library. Being in certain spots

every day hustlin'

MARK ANTHONY

Trixie proved to be a good if perhaps somewhat unconventional investment for me. Although she was a white trick, she knew a little bit about computers and the internet. And it was her idea that we go to a local library and use the internet to checkout the information that Squeeze had provided to us.

"Promise I think I got something that we can go off of." Trixie said while I nervously scoped out the library to make sure I wasn't being watched too closely by anybody.

"What're talkin' about?" I asked.

"Look. See all of this on the screen? Well I did a people search on Yahoo.com for all of the people with the last name Peterson that live in Camden, New Jersey and this is what came back."

"All of those fuckin' names!" I stated with disbelief and some disappointment. "How the hell are we gonna know which is the correct Peterson?"

"Well look at this." Trixie instructed while pointing at the computer monitor.

"We can kind of narrow it down by the ages. We should just start with all of the Petersons that are thirty and older. It's more likely that your daughter would be with a family in that age range, like I couldn't see the system putting her with some old ass family or someone that was too young," Trixie said.

"Ahight that makes some sense but then what?" I asked.

"Well now we need to pay for this info with a credit card to get the full addresses and telephone numbers and all of that," Trixie stated.

"Credit card? Bitch are you fuckin' stupid or what? I ain't

got no got damn credit cards! This is how you're supposed to be helping a nigga? Typing in shit like you a fuckin' Bill Gates computer whiz and shit! Trixie you ain't helping me and I need to find my daughter!" I said in a real vexed tone while not trying to attract too much attention.

"Look, you got $300 cash on you right?" Trixie asked.

"Yeah, give it to me and I'll get the info. Just watch me work."

I really had no choice but to trust that Trixie knew what the hell she was doing. I gave her the $300 and within a matter of minutes she had spotted a mark in the library. She found a middle aged white man and she explained him her plight and he agreed to let her use his credit card in exchange for the $100 fee that Trixie proposed.

"See, it's a safe website." Trixie explained. "It's $9.99 for every name that we search and I wanna search twenty names so they'll charge your credit card $200 and I'm giving you $300 so you are making $100 right off the top."

The white man thought about it for a moment and then he complied.

"It seems legitimate to me," he stated, pulling out his credit card while proceeding to type in the number.

"You know with so many identity theft things happening you have to be careful," he said.

Although the man had helped us out, I could sense that the real reason that he had helped was because he probably thought that he could kick it to Trixie in his own little middle-aged white way.

So to make sure that everything went over real smooth I

just made me feel way too uncomfortable and whenever I got that uncomfortable feeling I knew that it was time to bounce.

Before long we made our way to the Nissan and I let Trixie do the driving. And since she was from New Jersey she easily navigated her way to the New Jersey Turnpike.

"You think Squeeze was bullshitting with this information?" I asked Trixie.

Before she could answer the question I shot back with another question.

"Trixie you think we should park up the Nissan and just go rent sump'n? You think we pressing our luck in this ride right here?"

Trixie was ready to answer me but again I cut her off.

"Word to everything! If that nigga Squeeze is sending me on a wild goose chase I'll go back to New York and fuck that nigga up! Word is bond!"

I finally paused from my nervous barrage of questions and comments.

"You know him better than I do so I really don't know what to say. I mean I don't see why he would send you on some wild goose chase." Trixie reasoned.

I guess she was right and the fact was I really didn't have much to lose...

Underground Ho Spot, 1:30 a.m. Philadelphia, PA

"You sure this the spot?" Trixie asked.

"Yeah this is it. I know this area. He told me Old York Road, not too far from Temple University."

"What address did he give you?"

"He didn't, he just told me on Old York Road near Temple," I replied.

As Trixie navigated the car down Old York Road I was in search of Grams who had told me to meet him at Underground Ho Spot. Grams was my nigga that had let me rest at his spot in Philly for a few weeks after I had shot up the cops at Marissa's crib. He was also the one who was with me when we robbed Show and Squeeze at the Brooklyn Café.

I had contacted him while me and Trixie were on the New Jersey Turnpike because I figured he would know a little bit about Camden, New Jersey and the last thing I wanted to do was go up in Camden blind and not knowing what was what and fuck around and get bagged by the cops on a humble. So Grams had told me to meet him at the Ho Spot on Old York Road and we would build from there.

"This gotta be the spot." I said to Trixie as I had her park the car.

There was a slow stream of traffic coming from an apartment that was situated above a storefront. And I just knew that that had to be the spot.

"Ahight we gonna park here and you just follow my lead. I'm gonna play it off like you tricking tonight. Ahight?"

"Ok cool I gotchu." Trixie said, sounding like she was a black girl from Bed-Stuy and not some white whore from New Jersey.

As we approached what we hoped was the ho spot, Trixie spoke up.

"I gotchu Promise. But on the real I hate spots like this 'cause you gotta be careful as hell because spots like this are always getting raided." Trixie said. "That's why I never really worked them. The streets were always my thing. I'll walk the streets any day instead of being caged up in a spot like this waiting for undercover cops to come raid it."

"Shut da fuck up and move yo ass!" I yelled at Trixie.

I didn't need her talking all that bullshit about getting raided by cops, but I yelled at her even more so for the pimp and ho effect. As we had made our way up to the metal security door, a bodyguard looking cat came from inside the building and stepped outside to guard the building. And my yelling at Trixie made me look like I was her pimp who was getting her in line.

"What's good?" I asked the bodyguard looking dude.

He didn't respond to me and I didn't want to just straight out ask for Grams because I didn't know what was what at that point.

"What's the tip in and what's the tip out?" I asked.

After saying that the bodyguard looked at Trixie and he sort of relaxed his position.

"Who you wit'?" He asked.

"I'm wit' Grams."

The bodyguard nodded and then he asked, "How many girls you got? Just her?"

"Yeah just her."

"Ahight I'm a frisk y'all and then y'all just see my man right behind the security booth and make your way upstairs."

With that we were in. I went to the security booth and I asked about the tip in and out.

"It's just her with you?" The guy with the baldy behind the security glass asked.

"Yeah just her."

"Ahight let her go straight upstairs and she'll see a bathroom near the kitchen and she can go in there and get dressed up."

Trixie was a prostitute so she knew the ropes and she quickly went upstairs and did as she had been indirectly instructed.

As Trixie opened the heavy steel door that led to upstairs, the loud sound of thumping music rushed out at me.

Everyday I'm hustlin' hustlin' hustlin'...

The lyrics of the Rick Ross blasted in the background.

"Ahight with the tip in..." The bald guy behind the security booth said before he was interrupted.

"Oh shit my muthafuckin' nigga Promise! What's really good my nigga?" Grams yelled as he came up to me and gave me a pound.

"My nigga!" I said, as I was happier than a bitch to see Grams.

"Tip in? You brought some ho's wid ya?" Grams asked as I smiled. "Promise you is one hustlin' ass nigga! I thought you was coming to see about your daughter and this nigga is bringing hoes to the fucking spot!"

As a ho' came down stairs dressed in high heels and fishnet stockings you could here the music still thumping in the background.

Everyday I'm hustlin' hustlin' hustlin'…

Right on cue with the music I said to Grams, "Grams, everyday I'm hustlin', hustlin', hustlin'…"

The two of us laughed and then Grams took me to a back room on the first floor that looked like it doubled as a recording studio during the day. There were about three hoes in the room and each of them was giving someone a blowjob.

"That's you if you want it." Grams said.

At first I thought he was talking about one of the hoes but then I realized that he was referring to the lines of coke that were laid out on the table.

Normally just Chronic and Hennessy was what I fucked wit' but as stressed and anxious as I had been over my daughter I was ready to get high.

I sat down at the table and before I knew what was what - I had snorted two lines of coke. And after snorting it I reclined back in my chair closed my eyes and waited for the drug to do its thing.

Grams rolled a blunt and after sparking it he said, "So yo, where you resting at?"

Over the loud music I replied, "I'll probably just stay at a hotel near the airport tonight."

"Ahight so, I'm bouncing up outta here at about 5:00 in the morning. Just holla at me at like 12 in the afternoon and I'll scoop you up and we'll take it from there," Grams stated.

"100!" I replied as I gave Grams a pound and took like five pulls from the blunt.

I was definitely feeling high like a muthafucka as Grams

poured us both some Hennessy and we made our way upstairs.

When we got upstairs I saw a stream of hoes and most of them were choice pieces. There were also a bunch of dudes standing around getting wall dances and making propositions to the hoes.

"Look at this white bitch up in here butt ass naked!" Grams shouted in my ear.

"That's me!" I shouted back at Grams over the old school NWA gangsta rap track that was playing.

"Say word?"

"Word is bond!"

Grams started laughing as he said, "Promise you are about the grimiest nigga that I know!"

He continued to laugh as he said, "Promise you could have at least bought the bitch a pair of stiletto's or some stockings or something! Oh shit that is hilarious god! The bitch is walking around butt naked with a fucking pocketbook!"

I had to admit that Trixie did in fact look funny and out of place. Not that she didn't look sexy or appealing it was just that all of the other chicks were walking around in thongs, or something provocative and sexy looking, with make up on and all of that. And Trixie was white as a mouse walking around with literally no clothes on and it just looked wild as hell. Her toenails weren't even painted. It was an underground spot and anything goes.

The thing was I had never planned on pimpin' Trixie it was just something that just happened. But with the coke, weed, and liquor flowing through my body I was open as hell and the thought of Trixie getting me some money was sounding like music to my ears.

The DJ switched up the track and put on a Jay-Z track. The record *Can I Get A Fuck You* was booming in the room as Trixie spotted Grams and me and walked over to us.

"What's up?" Trixie asked.

"What's up?" I replied with a disgusted look on my face. "You better get this money that's what's up!" I replied.

I totally caught Trixie off guard with my demeanor and she looked at me kind of confused.

"Don't stand around looking at me bitch! Get this money!" I shouted over the music. Trixie looked at me and she walked off and sort of began to follow the lead of the other hoes. And before long she was walking off with a nigga ready to service him in one of the back rooms...

By the time we left the spot it was just about 5 in the morning and Trixie had done good. In the span of about four hours she had made about $450, which she had no problem handing over to me.

"Promise at least you could have told me that you wanted me to trick for you? You did it on some ol' chump as nigga shit," Trixie said as we piled into the Nissan.

I was feeling like I was hung-over even though I hadn't drunk that much. So I wasn't really in the mood for much of Trixie's bullshit. I was gonna flip on her but at the same time I was sensible enough to realize that I needed her to help me get my daughter.

"Pull out and make a left at the corner and then make another left at the first light."

I ignored Trixie's comment as I was feeling like I was ready to throw up.

"We gotta make our way to the Hilton over near the airport." I added.

Trixie remained calm and quiet as we navigated through the dark Philadelphia streets.

"On the real I wasn't planning on you getting us no money tonight. It just happened. Make a left right there and get on the interstate and you'll see the signs for the airport. Follow those signs and you'll see a bunch of hotels. Just exit near the hotels and navigate your way to the Hilton. My ass is feeling sick and I gotta go to sleep," I stated as I reclined in my chair and went to sleep.

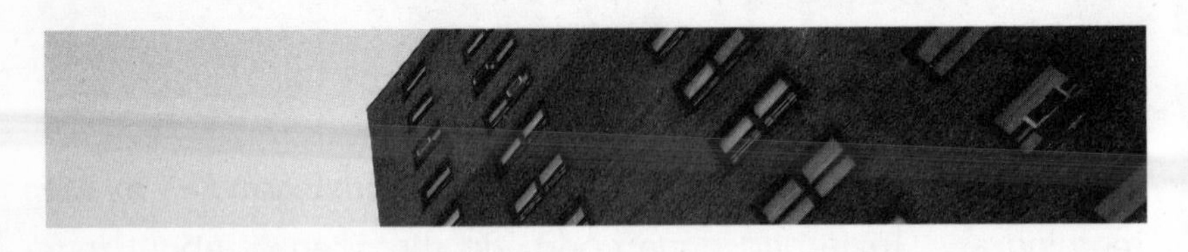

1:30 p.m. Camden, New Jersey
USA Homicide Capital

Grams had met us at the Hilton and he suggested that we call the phone numbers that we had and try to narrow down the search for Ashley even more. It was an excellent idea and that was when Trixie's white accent came in good for us. She dialed number after number and asked if she could speak to Ashley. And with each call my hope began to fade as caller after caller claimed that no one by the name of Ashley lived at the residence. It wasn't until the 16th call made that we felt we were onto something.

Trixie had the phone on speakerphone mode as she asked, "Hello may I speak with Ashley?"

"Ashley?" The person on the other end asked sounding somewhat curious. "May I ask who is calling and what this is in reference to?"

"Oh, I'm sorry," Trixie replied. "This is Nikki. I'm a friend of Ashley's we were in the same dorm at college last year and I no longer go to that college anymore so I was just calling to say hello, actually to surprise Ashley and to talk about old times," Trixie said and I immediately knew where she was going with her line of talk.

"Oh." The party on the other line stated. "I think you have the wrong number."

"Doesn't Ashley live at this address?" Trixie asked as I was prepared for yet another let down.

"Yes Ashley lives here but she is way too young for college so I think you may have dialed the wrong number," the person said.

"Oh, I am so sorry. I got this number from off the internet."

"It's not a problem," the lady replied before hanging up.

My heart was racing a mile a minute as I said, "That's it! I know she's there."

Grams asked to see the address and then he quickly stated that he was almost sure he knew where the address was located.

"If that is where I think it is, on the real it don't get no more ghetto than that area! Word! Camden is as wild as it gets. It's the murder capital in the country but that particular part of Camden is the fuckin' slums!" Grams informed us.

I thought for a minute in silence. Breaking my silence I said, "This what we'll do. I don't wanna take a chance driving the Nissan so we'll go to the airport rent a car and head over to Camden and scope everything out before we make any moves."

"Baby, we can't rent a car without a credit card," Trixie replied.

"She's right, Promise," Grams added. "But yo we'll be ahight let's just roll in my ride."

We all piled into Grams all Black quarter to eight BMW. A car that he informed me he was able to get thanks to the robbery that we had committed at the Brooklyn Café.

"Promise that's why you'll always be my nigga fo' life. You attract money like a magnet," he stated.

In a matter of minutes we were in Camden and it didn't take long to see what Grams had been talking about. Being from New York, I had seen my share of Ghettos. But Southside Jamaica, Queens, Brownsville, Brooklyn, or the South Bronx all couldn't touch Camden, New Jersey in terms of slum ghetto-ness. The shit looked worse than the slums of Baltimore, Maryland.

"I can't believe the system got my daughter growing up in this shit! They would have never have done that to no white kid!" I yelled, careless that Trixie was white.

"This the block," Grams said as he pulled in front of a local store.

The store sat at the corner of a two-block stretch of stores and it ran perpendicular to the block that we suspected Ashley was on. There were a number of people out on the strip who looked as if they were just going about their business.

"The house is probably about midway down the block if we make a right turn here," Grams stated.

"Okay cool," I said. "But what we gotta do is circle the block one time and look for anything that looks suspicious. And then we wait about a half hour and do the exact same thing before we make any kind of moves. The last thing that I want is for the Feds to be staking out my daughter's joint and I get this close to her and get knocked!"

Grams complied with my instructions and he started up the car and we made a right turn onto the block and cruised down the block in what was a normal driving pace for a residential block.

"Y'all see anything?" Grams asked.

"Nah everything looks cool," I replied.

"That's the house right there, the brick one on the left!" Trixie informed us.

My palms were sweaty from my nerves that were not at ease with all that I knew about stick-ups and running up in niggas cribs and doing robberies. I was more than ready to walk up to the door with my .45 and do my thing and come out with my daughter.

"You think she's home?" Grams asked.

"Yeah." I quickly replied as I hoped for the best and as thoughts of Ashley's mom popped into my head.

"How we gonna do this?" Grams asked.

Trixie stated that she could walk up to the door and act like she was at the wrong address just to get a feel for what the house looked like on the inside and to see who was home. But we thought that that would raise too many red flags since we had already called and asked for an Ashley. That would have made things look way too suspicious.

"We gonna have to come back tonight when it gets dark and run up in that bitch," I said.

Knowing that it was always very risky to run up in someone's house without knowing what or who was inside, I felt safer doing something like that when it was dark outside.

As Grams made two right turns and was headed back towards the direction of the store that we had been parked in front of he stated, "Did y'all see that Escalade that was parked all the way at the end of the block? It was just before we made the right turn at the end of the block that Ashley's house is on. That was the only thing that looked outta place to me. That whip don't belong here," Grams stated.

"Nah I didn't see it but why you say that?" I asked. "You be around here like that to know what niggas is driving? Maybe some nigga is just hustlin' and got dough and his girl lives on the block," I reasoned.

Grams didn't say anything and neither did Trixie.

"Let's go get some McDonald's and then we can circle back but lets just come up the block from the opposite direction so we won't draw no attention to ourselves," I stated.

As we made it to the McDonalds drive thru window Grams said, "Them Feds be driving them high end whips and be trippin' up muthafuckas so that's why my radar went up."

Grams was street, so if that's what he was suspecting then I trusted and respected his instincts and his gangsta and I knew that we had to proceed with caution. My nerves were now so on edge that I couldn't even bring myself to eat.

As I sat and waited for Trixie and Grams to finish their food I wondered if Ashley still liked McDonald's and I wondered when was the last time she'd been to McDonald's. Buying Ashley a McDonald's happy meal quickly became another motivator for me. Tonight, I told myself, the first thing that I'm gonna do is buy Ashley a Happy Meal. Word!

Grams and Trixie were finally finished eating and Grams started up the car and made his way back to what we still hoped was Ashley's block.

When we were about two blocks away Grams turned down the music and said, "The Escalade is gonna be on the passenger side of our ride if it's still there. We'll just roll through at a normal speed and we can look as hard as we want to at them 'cause they can't see through the tints on this whip."

As we came up on the Escalade the first thing that Trixie noticed was that the Escalade had Pennsylvania plates. And that made me think even more that it was probably not the Feds because the Feds would have likely have had New Jersey plates.

"So what?" Grams questioned. "Who cares about the plates, I wanna know who is inside the muthafucka."

We passed the Escalade and chills ran down my body and so did rage and anger.

"Sonnofabitch!" I screamed.

"What's up? What?" Both Trixie and Grams asked as Grams continued to drive.

"That bitch ass nigga Squeeze played my ass!" I yelled.

"What happened?" Grams asked.

"That dude in the Escalade is Tooks, the OG from New York!" I explained.

Trixie and Grams pressed me for more of an explanation.

"Chill! Just give me a fucking minute to think!" I yelled.

All sorts of thoughts ran through my head. I wanted to know exactly what was Tooks doing on the same block that I thought Ashley lived on? Maybe Audrey had someone in her family go into the foster care system and located Ashley so that Ashley would be in good hands? Maybe Ashley didn't even live on this block at all and I was in fact on a wild goose chase? I was really starting to trip out.

I finally began to explain to Grams and Trixie exactly who Tooks was and how he had swore to fuck my ass up if things went south with Audrey his niece. And then I had to re-explain everything that went down between me an Audrey.

"So where is the connection to Squeeze and Tooks?" Grams asked.

"I don't know. But this ain't no coincidence!" I replied. "Ain't no way."

Trixie butted her skinny white-ass in.

"This don't seem right because Squeeze never straight up gave you Ashley's address. We found that shit by narrowing it down from a bunch of possible names. So I don't see how it's connecting," Trixie added.

She had a good point. And she continued on.

"Ashley has to be at this address because what are the chances that Tooks would be here on this block especially if Squeeze never gave you the exact address. The only way that you and Tooks could have ended up on this same block is if there is a common thing between you and Tooks on this block and that common thing is Ashley your daughter."

Trixie was right but I didn't need this complication. I was nervous as hell and didn't know what to do but I couldn't leave Camden without at least knocking on that door and checking for my daughter. But if I moved too quickly I knew that I could be walking into a booby trap.

Why the fuck is Tooks in a Escalade with Pennsylvania plates? I asked myself. I also didn't know who the other dude was that Tooks was with.

"This the deal, we saw them and I know they don't know my whip or who is in this car so we got the upper hand right now. We need to move on them niggas. I say we drive by they shit and spray the bitch up with slugs. Shoot first and ask questions later." Grams reasoned.

Tooks ain't working with no Feds I told myself. Ain't no way, unless it's some kind of deal to spring Audrey by him helping the Feds to catch me. I had to stop thinking like that. But it was hard. I didn't want to believe that Squeeze would do me like this but at the same time I had to remember that this was the streets and anything goes. I also remembered how Squeeze acted real shady when I showed up that night at the Brooklyn Café with Marissa. Of course I had robbed his ass and made him get butt-naked. Maybe this was his way of getting revenge.

"Fuck this shit! Grams pull over," I ordered.

Grams pulled to the side of the road and I climbed in the back seat with Trixie and I instructed her to climb into the front seat. We had switched positions in the car without actually exiting the car simply because I didn't want any attention being drawn to ourselves.

"This the plan and I need y'all niggas to just ride wit' me

and follow what the fuck I say. Listen real close cuz we can't make no mistakes. If we make a mistake with Tooks he'll light our asses up!" I said.

"No doubt." Grams stated.

"Grams we gonna drive down the block so that the drivers' side of our car will be next to the passenger side of their car," I instructed.

"Okay," Grams replied.

"Now, Trixie, while we're driving I want you to start sucking Grams dick. Suck it like you trying to win sump'n."

"Hmm," Trixie hummed.

"Grams while she's busy wid your Jimmie, I want you to have your gun sandwiched in between the driver's door and the side of the drivers' seat where nobody can see it, have your right hand on the steering wheel. Trixie here, take this," I said handing Trixie a loaded .45.

"What's this for?" She asked.

"This gun is gonna be under Grams lap and will be visible only to you. Just keep sucking his dick and don't stop. I'm gonna be laying on the floor in the back with my .45 in my hand. What we gonna do is roll up next to the Escalade and Grams you do the talking. Roll down your window with Trixie still sucking your Johnson. Start telling Tooks that your ho's scared to walk the block because she thinks they're po-po. And once you say, 'See Trixie they ain't cops,' that's when I'll jump out and run up on Tooks and his people before they know what's what."

"Sounds good," Grams said.

"Grams I want you to draw your gun on them. Trixie I want you to grab the .45 from under Grams lap and aim that shit at the

Escalade like you ready to lay a nigga out...! Y'all got it?" I asked after having given the longwinded instructions.

"Ahight, I'm ready for all that suckin'," Grams said.

"Yeah the plan is good," Trixie concurred.

"Grams on the real, this is a real live ass nigga. As live as they come, so if you see anything not looking right don't hesitate to bust a nigga. If y'all see anybody running from the Escalade then bust a cap up in they ass. Trixie when me and Grams draw our guns and you get the gun that is on Grams' lap I want you to immediately look around to make sure that there ain't nobody across the street, in another car or walking down the block that might be with Tooks. If you see anything like that, just start shooting first and asking questions later. Ahight?"

"Ahight," Trixie nodded.

I could sense that she was nervous. She was also probably questioning how did she wind up in my gangsta plans. Grams looked uneasy but I think that was because he wasn't sure if Tooks was in the truck with a cop or if there were other cops right on that same block waiting to swarm in.

After me and Trixie switched positions I was thankful that the 745 had a lot of room in the back. I crouched down in the back and was basically laying in a disjointed fetal position. With the dark tints, I was confident that Tooks wouldn't be able to see a thing until it was too late.

"Y'all good up there?" I asked as I finally had fidgeted into a comfortable position and at that point I wasn't moving anymore.

"Yes sir, I'm good," Grams replied.

Then he started to chuckle as he said, "I've been in some shit on the street and I've seen some shit go down on the street but

I ain't never run up on nobody while getting a blowjob! Word!"

We all started laughing. I heard Grams unzip his pants.

"I gotta pull my pants down a little bit so that it'll be no question that I'm getting a blowjob. And plus it'll help hide the gun that's in my lap," Grams stated.

"Trixie, you ahight?" I asked.

"Yeah, I'm okay," she said. "Grams you better not be a one minute man because I puts it down with my head game!" she added lightening the mood.

Everyone in the car laughed at Trixie's comment and I felt good that the tension had been broken. As I thought, only in the hood would somebody be plotting on a nigga while getting a blowjob. But that was how brilliant I knew I had to be if I was gonna go at Tooks. Before I knew what was what I could hear Trixie in the front seat slurping on Grams joint.

"Grams, do I take care of you or what? You got twenty something G's with me last time and now you getting some head in the whip."

"Oh shit! On the real Trixie your head game is sick! You gonna make it hard for a nigga to focus," Grams excitedly exclaimed, obviously enjoying the blowjob.

Trixie sounded as if she'd come up for some air and then she laughed and before long she went back to sucking off Grams.

"Ahight, we rollin'," Grams said as he put the car in drive and headed towards the Escalade.

"Cool. Grams just make sure all of the doors is unlocked," I said as my heartrate was beginning to pick up.

I could hear the front windows being rolled down on the

BMW and I felt the air that quickly filled up the car and I knew that we had to be just about right up on the Escalade. Then the car stopped. I could hear Trixie still slobbing and slurping away.

"My man! My man can you roll down the window for a second?" Grams shouted from his window.

There was an awkward pause and silence and I wondered what the hell was going on.

"What's up fella?" Grams asked.

"Everything's everything partner," Tooks stated in his OG accent.

Grams was quiet and I was hoping that he didn't front on me.

"Oh shit! Ah... Ol' up a minute baby," Grams grunted.

He sounded like he was talking to Trixie. Trixie seemed as if she had come back up for some air. Mentally I was screaming because they were already not following the plan.

"No disrespect. It'd help a nigga out if the two of y'all wasn't posted up on the block just chillin' like fucking po'-po'. You feelin' me?" Grams stated.

Cool, I said to myself. I was digging Grams' flow. Then right on cue I heard Trixie's mouth slobbing his dick. Her timing was perfect.

Tooks had made no reply to Grams comment and neither did anyone else inside the Escalade.

Grams went on, "I got my girls scared to come and work on the block cuz they don't know who y'all are. I mean y'all are a block away from the strip but my bitches ain't comfortable with y'all sitting here."

"It's cool," Tooks responded.

Then there was an awkward pause. It was like did Tooks mean it was cool in the sense that they would drive off or did he just mean it was cool in the sense of he wasn't a cop? Grams flow had left him. Trixie must have sensed it too. She stopped sucking on Grams dick and spoke up and asked Tooks if she could go for a ride in his truck.

"Nah, sweetheart we good. You seem like you got your hands full already," Tooks replied.

"What about your man? He don't wanna go for a ride with me around the block?" Trixie asked.

Tooks didn't respond and Trixie went back to sucking on Grams dick.

"Get ya' money partner we from outta town and we ain't trying to knock nobody's hustle. We just waiting on our man," Tooks explained.

"No doubt," Grams replied. "Just making sure y'all ain't fucking Feds."

There was no reply from anyone in the Escalade.

"See Trixie, I told you they ain't fuckin' cops," Grams remarked.

That was my cue. Without hesitation I sat up with the quickness, busting out of the BMW and like a jackrabbit I was up on the Escalade, my .45 aimed at Tooks' dome.

Grams was also scrambling to get out of the car. He had his gun in one hand pointed at the Escalade. And with his other hand he was trying to pull up his pants and cover his exposed erection.

"What da fuck's da deal, Tooks!" I shouted.

Tooks held his hands up in an act of surrender. Obviously

off guard, he was shook.

"Nigga if you even flinch I'll murder yo ass!" I shouted at Tooks's boy who was in the driver's seat.

He was about to make a move for his gun. There were some people on the block and they saw the guns that we had drawn and while some people quickly got outta dodge, there were other hood rats that had to come rushing towards the excitement. Trixie gotta out the BMW and had her gun pointed on the hood rats rushing to see what was going on.

"This ain't a party people! Get the fuck outta here!" She barked at the onlookers while aiming her gun at them.

At that point Grams had pulled his pants up and had made it to the driver's side of the Escalade.

"Both of y'all get the fuck out!" I ordered.

"Tooks this is a young man's game, baby! You too old to play ball now my nigga!" I boasted. Tooks was right where I wanted him and he knew it.

"Look young blood. You and your partner need to calm the fuck down!" Tooks yelled. He and his partner reluctantly got out of the Cadillac.

"Shut the fuck up!" Grams barked.

"Get in the back!" I ordered. "Trixie you drive the BMW and follow us. Grams you drive the Escalade and I'll keep my heat on these niggas."

Before complying with my wishes Grams showed his street smarts by telling me to hold up. He quickly frisked both Tooks and his boy then he looked under the seats. All obvious and visible areas in the Escalade were checked to make sure that there was no guns or weapons or cellphones.

"We good!" Grams relayed to me.

With that, we ordered Tooks and his man to get inside the truck. We were out. Trixie was following right behind.

"Promise that's your fuckin' problem! You're a got-damn hot-headed sonnofabitch!" Tooks scowled as he looked at me with disgust.

"Nigga fuck you!" I replied. "What the hell are you doing out here?"

"What am I doing out here? I'm visiting your daughter! I'm the one who's been putting food in her mouth ever since you had my niece locked up! That's what I'm doing out here!" Tooks replied with convincing disgust, but at the same time I could tell that he didn't have his usual confident street-swagger in his voice.

"That's bullshit!" I shouted as I continued to face the backseats while holding my gun on Tooks and his man.

I knew exactly how to call his bluff. "Squeeze put you on to me and my daughter and yo ass is out here gunning for me!"

Tooks was silent and his silence had sealed his fate. In my heart I knew I had guessed right. And even if I was wrong the fact remained that Tooks was a big threat to my existence and I knew that you don't pull a gun on a man like Tooks and not use it.

"Listen Promise..." Tooks' man began to talk and I immediately cut him off.

"Nigga, did I tell you to open your mouth? You don't even know me dude!" I yelled.

"Johnny, it's okay." Tooks said in an attempt to ease the tensions.

For Audrey's sake I hated to do what I was about to do. But I was too close to seeing my daughter and being reunited with her and starting over, I just couldn't let Tooks be a threat to that hope I had. It was like the only hope I had and I was feeling desperate like an animal that was cornered and getting beat.

Blaadow! Blaadow! Was the deafening sound that came from the .45 that I was holding. I had pumped two shots into Tooks' head and his body immediately lay limp and lifeless.

Blaadow! The third shot from my gun managed to hit Johnny right in the throat and he immediately grabbed and clutched his throat. He had one of the wildest most panicked looks on his face. It's a look that I know is gonna haunt me in the future. It's a look that you can't describe. It's a look that only a human that knows that they are about to die can muster up.

As blood flowed and squirted out of Johnny's neck, Grams managed to maneuver our way back to Philly. And before long, Johnny had stopped clutching his throat and his body lay as limp as an 80 year old dick while his eyes rolled to the back of his head.

I rolled down the window and instructed Trixie to go to a gas station and to purchase some gasoline and to put some inside of whatever type of container that she could find.

"Put it in soda can if you have to." I yelled. "I don't care what you put it in, and then follow us."

"Grams I just killed one of the wildest muthafuckas from Harlem!" I said as the reality of what I'd done began to set in.

"You did what you had to do. If you didn't pop that nigga he would have made it his life mission to come after me and you until he murdered us" Gram accurately stated.

"Word is bond! But you know what? Took was too old for this shit! I mean I hate to see the nigga shot up like that 'cause

I got respect for the game and nothing but love for his niece but at the same time only the strong survive, and I ain't no weak muthafucka." I stated with heavy street confidence, all the while on the inside I was shitting bricks.

Trixie had purchased the gas and then quickly followed Grams and me as Grams maneuvered the Escalade to a desolated area. The two of us quickly got out and retrieved the gasoline from Trixie that she had placed inside of a gallon size milk container.

Grams doused the inside of the Escalade with gasoline and also poured gasoline on the roof and hood of the Escalade before tossing a match inside the truck and setting it a blaze. The three of us jumped inside the BMW and waited until the fire was fully engulfing the inside of the Escalade and then we sped off.

There were hardly any words spoken between the three of us for obvious reasons. I mean all of that gung-ho gun toting shoot em' up shit that you see in the mafia movies where cats kill somebody and then go and chill with their family like everything is all good, well that ain't how it really goes down.

It goes down like it was going down inside of that BMW for the three of us. You feel like shit and like the scum of the earth after taking another human being's life. And that was the reason silence covered us like a blanket. I was able to break the silence by telling Grams that I was sorry for having roped him into that whole murder shit. I had definitely not planned for things to go that way but that was how things played themselves out.

"Dude, on the real. As soon as I get my hands on some real cake I'm a come see a nigga and hit you off wit' like 10G's for this shit. Word!" I emphatically proclaimed and I meant every word of it.

Grams downplayed everything but that was the type of cat he was. Real street, but real humble at the same time.

"What's the deal with your daughter?" Grams asked.

I shook my head and then blew some air out of my lungs.

"Tonight I gotta make my move and get her. I'm just running up in the crib and the only way I ain't coming out with her is if they take me out of that crib in a body bag," I said and paused.

"But Grams, we got it from here. Just take us back to the hotel and let us pick up the whip and me and Trixie will head back to Camden on our own. You already did more than enough. We got this shit from here."

"Promise I got your back. Just say the word. It ain't nothing," Grams replied.

I knew that he would have my back but on the real all I needed at that point was for Trixie to ride shotgun in the Nissan and I was gonna get my daughter. There was no need for help at that point.

"You sure you gonna be aight?" Grams asked again as we pulled up to the Nissan.

"No doubt, I got this," I replied as the BMW sat idling next to the Nissan.

"I gotta move tonight and get Ashley as soon as it gets dark. This whole shit with Tooks, it kinda got my ass spooked and I just wanna get the hell up outta here and start over."

After that there was nothing but silence in the car. Then Grams turned on the radio to break the awkward silence.

"Turn the music down for a second," I requested.

"Grams on the real, this is what I need you to do for me..." I said as I took a long pause. "If I get killed tonight or if I get bagged by the cops..."

Grams cut me off. "Promise, c'mon with that nonsense."

"Nah, this is real talk! Word! If I get killed or bagged, just promise me this one thing. Wait for shit to die down and when it does, I need you to tell my daughter that I love her and that I miss her and that I don't want her to be afraid or scared of anything."

I had to watch myself because I was beginning to get real emotional.

"Promise, you got my word on that," Grams said.

There was another pause as I reached into my pocket.

"Here, make sure that she also gets this." I instructed as I handed Grams a passport photo of myself that I had taken at a Walgreens drugstore in Brooklyn.

"No doubt," Grams replied. "I'll lookout for her like she was one of mines... But you know what? Everything's gonna be ahight, kid."

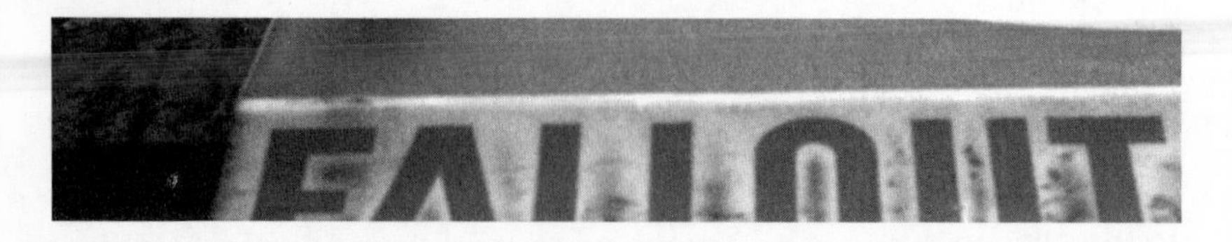

Camden, New Jersey 11:00 p.m.

I was beyond tired and was tired for good reason. The night before, I had been in a whorehouse drinking liquor and sniffing coke until five in the morning and then with only a few hours of sleep I had been drained from all my energy with my current day's activities, which included killing two gangsters in cold blood, and then torching the incriminating evidence.

But now wasn't the time for no tiredness. I had one objective to complete and then I could hopefully move on with my life. That objective was to get my daughter.

I had Trixie park right in front of the house that Ashley was staying in. There was gonna be no casing the house and trying to figure shit out. My mind was already made up to just march right into the joint and get my daughter, even if it meant someone had to get killed in the process.

"Trixie keep the car running and keep it in drive with your foot on the brake pedal. And when I come out with Ashley and hop in, you don't ask no questions and you don't hesitate. You just floor this bitch and get the fuck up outta dodge as quick as you can. Okay?"

Trixie nodded her head.

"I said, okay?" I reiterated because I wanted Trixie to formally acknowledge my words with more than just a head nod.

"Yeah okay," she finally responded.

With that I tucked my .45 in my waistband and exited from the car. I blew a whole lot of anxious air from my lungs and walked towards the yard to where Ashley was staying.

The yard looked a mess and there were two sickly looking stray dogs that were in the front yard along with broken dirty toys that were strewn across the mangled patchy grass. I noticed that all of the lights seemed to be on inside the house, which was a good thing, I guess.

I didn't know what I was gonna say once I knocked on the door. I didn't know if I was gonna play it off like I was lost and needed directions or if I was gonna say that my car had broke down and that I needed to use their phone. I wasn't sure. I had even contemplated just walking up to the door and asking for Ashley. Just be natural I said to myself as I knocked three times on the door.

"Auntie Angie somebody's at the door," a high-pitched little girl's voice yelled.

I was certain that that was my little girl. My heart was racing and I couldn't wait to see if that in fact was her. Becoming more and more impatient, I knocked three more times on the door.

"Just a minute, I'm coming," the lady inside the house yelled with a bit of an attitude.

There was no screen door so when the lady came to the door and opened it she and I were face to face.

My eyes immediately got wide. And I was sure that she could see my chest rise from inhaling and then deflate from exhaling.

"Yes...? Can I help you?" The lady asked as she sort of positioned her body behind the door and let only her head be visible.

I thought about pushing in the door but I quickly decided against.

"Yeah I am so sorry to bother you miss but my car broke down and I was just wondering if I could use your phone to call Triple A." I said as I was hoping that I was being convincing enough.

The lady looked at me with much suspicion and she hesitated before saying anything.

"I mean you don't have to let me inside. If you have a cordless phone or a cellphone you could bring it to me," I added for good measure.

The lady still looked unconvinced. And just as I was about to reach into my waistband and pull out my gun and rush the door, a little hand appeared near the doorknob. The little hand didn't actually grip the doorknob. Instead it gripped the door and attempted to pull it open.

"Ashley, go upstairs to your room!" The woman ordered.

My eyes got wide like a drug addict and I instinctively reached for the door and slightly pushed it but not in a threatening way. That was my daughter and I needed to see her at that moment.

"I wanna see," Ashley said ignoring the woman's orders and pulled at the door attempting to open it.

It was almost like she knew I was at the door or something.

Promise push open the fucking door and grab Ashley and be out nigga! I wanted to yell to myself.

Finally Ashley was able to make some headway and she snaked her head around the door and her beautiful face was now in my full view. She just looked so beautiful and she looked as if she'd gotten so big. I wanted to melt right there on the spot!

"Daddy!" Ashley yelled.

A Kool Aid smile splashed across my face, as I was happy as hell that Ashley still remembered me. She began to struggle with all her might to get from behind the door.

"Daddy?" The woman questioned.

At that point I knew that I had to make my move and grab Ashley and be out.

"Baby, who is that at the fucking door this time of night?" A deep sounding male voice shouted from inside the house.

"Daddy! Daddy!" Ashley yelled again with more excitement in her voice as she violently tried to get to me.

Fuck this! I said to myself as I pushed the door in while simultaneously reaching for my .45

"Come on Ashley! Daddy's here!" I said and drew my gun.

My finger was on the trigger itching and ready to blast anybody that tried to stop me from taking my daughter...

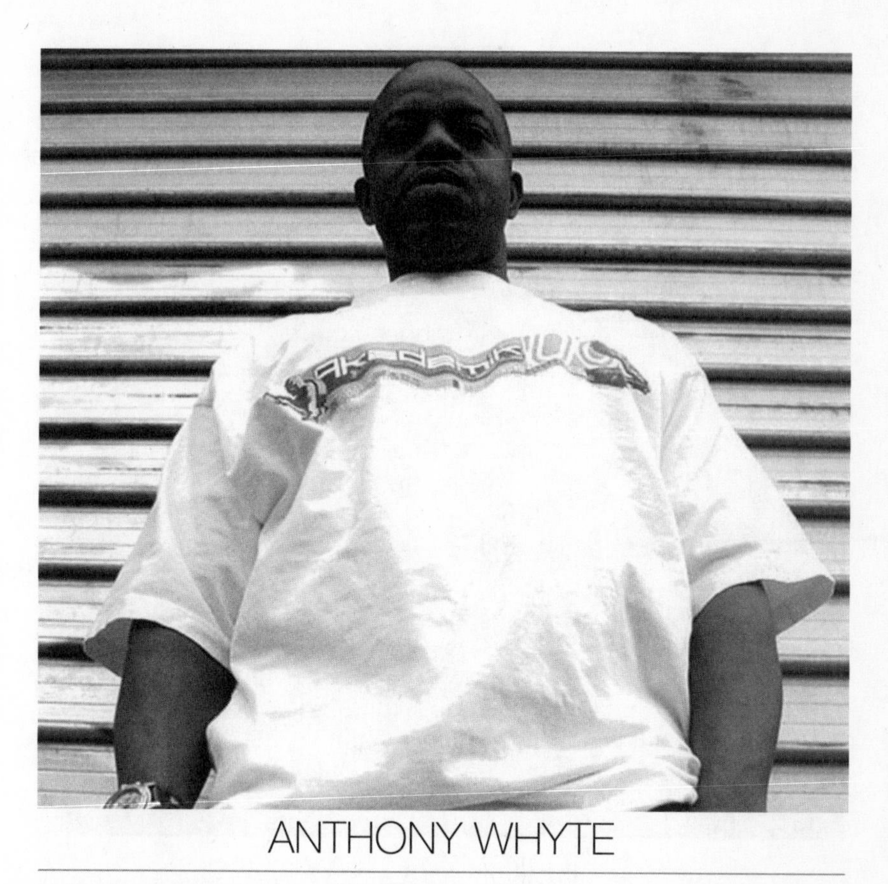

ANTHONY WHYTE

He's the master of this literary domain, holding the book game down like it was his kingdom. Author of the classic, Ghetto Girls Series, editor and CEO of Augustus Publishing, the hottest on the book scene. A true pioneer and leader, Whyte's style has been copied never duplicated. He's way ahead of his time. In grand steeze, he continues to reign. Since '96 when he coined the phrase, Hip Hop Literature, Whyte has been forever bringing reading back to real life.

Hit up Anthony Whyte at www.streetlitreview.com

ERICK S GRAY

Known as Mr. Prolifick, this young and very talented storyteller is honing his skills as a legend in the book game. He's written classics such as the exciting erotica, Booty Call *69 and the best fiction and award winning, gangster saga, Crave All... Lose All. Hailing from South Side. Jamaica, Queens, Mr. Prolifick goes hard for his on the STREETS OF NEW YORK.

Hit up Erick S Gray at www.streetlitreview.com

MARK ANTHONY

The author and publisher is a talented veteran of the book game. Reppin' Q-Boro, the publishing house he started and the area he's from. Mark Anthony has conquered the publishing world while writing several stories of grit and grime... from Paper Chasers to Ladies' Nite, his style definitely appeals to readers of all sex, especially to the ladies.

Hit up Mark Anthony at www.streetlitreview.com

GHETTO GIRLS IV

Young Luv

ESSENCE BESTSELLING AUTHOR
ANTHONY WHYTE

Ghetto Girls IV Young Luv
$14.95 // 9780979281662

Ghetto Girls
$14.95 // 0975945319

Ghetto Girls Too
$14.95 // 0975945300

Ghetto Girls 3 Soo Hood
$14.95 // 0975945351

THE BEST OF THE STREET CHRONICLES TODAY, THE **GHETTO GIRLS SERIES** IS A WONDERFULLY HYPNOTIC ADVENTURE THAT DELVES INTO THE CONVOLUTED MINDS OF CRIMINALS AND THE DARK WORLD OF POLICE CORRUPTION. YET, THERE IS SOMETHING THRILLING AND SURPRISINGLY TENDER ABOUT THIS ONGOING YOUNG-ADULT SAGA FILLED WITH MAD FLAVA.

Love and a Gangsta

author // **ERICK S GRAY**

This explosive sequel to **Crave All Lose All**. Soul and America were together ten years 'til Soul's incarceration for drugs. Faithfully, she waited four years for his return. Once home they find life ain't so easy anymore. America believes in holding her man down and expects Soul to be as committed. His lust for fast money rears its ugly head at the same time America's music career takes off. From shootouts, to hustling and thugging life, Soul and his man, Omega, have done it. Omega is on the come-up in the drug-game of South Jamaica, Queens. Using ties to a Mexican drug cartel, Omega has Queens in his grip. His older brother, Rahmel, was Soul's cellmate in an upstate prison. Rahmel, a man of God, tries to counsel Soul. Omega introduces New York to crystal meth. Misery loves company and on the road to the riches and spoils of the game, Omega wants the only man he can trust, Soul, with him. Love between Soul and America is tested by an unforgivable greed that leads quickly to deception and murder.

$14.95 // 9780979281648

Enjoy this excerpt from **Love and a Gangsta**
a novel by Erick S. Gray

IN STORES NOW!

America

2006 Jamaica, Queens

Finally the day I thought about for four long years was here. In the shower, the water cascading off my brown skin, thinking about his touch made my nipples swell in anticipation. I remember his hands caressing me night after night. My thoughts left my thighs shaking in excitement

I wanted to be oh so fresh for him. I kept myself pure for years just because I love him. My girlfriends thought that I was crazy, going without dick for so long. When you're strongly in love with a man why fuck another. I was longing for only one to be inside me. The thought of him coming back to me soon was sexual satisfying. Don't get me wrong, I love sex, but if it wasn't with Omar, then I was cool and did without until he returned.

Omar captured my heart the very first time we met. He was from the streets, but had a strong aura and I accepted him. Soon afterwards, he took my virginity and I wanted to have his babies.

On the streets, he was known as Soul. He rapped, played the piano, and the guitar. His musical gifts were phenomenal and he was a great dancer. Soul played basketball like he belonged in the pros. Most of all, he was a gentlemen. Despite his street reputation, my baby knew how to take care of me inside and outside the bedroom.

Omar wasn't perfect. Like every other man on this planet, he had flaws. The streets possessed him, and sometimes hustling and hanging with his homeboys got in the way of his talents.

Soul was a crack dealer. He got into too many fights. He drank too much. A rumor was floating around the hood that he was cheating on me. I looked beyond his bad qualities and wanted us to be together forever. Soul was my first, and I wanted him to be my last.

I met him when I was fifteen and he was seventeen. Back then he'd hangout with his boys in front of the bodega on the corner of Supthin and South Road. Soul was hustling and getting into trouble like all the youths on the corner.

He was cute and his style was different from his peers. They wore their pants low and sagging off their butts, but Omar rocked khakis and wore his jeans with a belt. They sported Timberlands, but you would catch my baby in Gucci loafers or soft bottom shoes, sometimes he would wear a suit and wing tips. While his friends wore cornrows, Omar took a trip to the barbershop once a week and kept his low shadow in style. His boys wore jewelry like they took advice from Mr. T. Omar sported a thin gold chain and a small cross his mother had given him.

One cool summer day, Omar bumped into me as I was coming out of the bodega carrying groceries for my aunt. We locked eyes briefly. I remained silent and walked passed the same group of boys who lingered in front of the store on the daily. I was walking down the block and heard someone running behind me. Startled, I spun around and saw Omar jogging up to me.

"Hey hold up, youngin'."

"Youngin'?" I snapped. "Please, you're barely older than me."

"Yo, let me carry that for you," he chuckled.

"Why?" I answered reluctantly.

"It would be the polite thing to do. Besides, you're too small to be carrying that huge bag."

"I was doing fine for half a block without your help. Does it look like I'm struggling?"

"Yo, you got some mouth. How old are you?" He smiled.

"Old enough."

"You feisty, girl. I like that," he countered.

"Whateva!" I said, walking away.

Omar was persistent. He then said, "Being a man, I'm not going to let you carry these bags to your crib by yourself. My mama raised me better than that."

"Oh, she did, huh? And did she teach you about harassment too?"

"Harassment? Yo, why you coming at me like that, shorty? I'm just tryin' to help you?"

I stared at him with a grim look.

"You don't trust me, huh? I look like a guy who's gonna take your bag, huh?" He asked with the warmest smile. It spread from ear to ear and was contagious.

"See, there's that smile I was lookin' for."

"Oh just shut up about it," I joked.

He took the bags from me and we walked side by side to my home. I was attracted to the swagger of this lanky six-foot frame cut with six-pack abs and nice arms. He wore denim shorts, wife-beater, sporting new red and white Jordan's.

"So what's your name, beautiful?"

His onyx eyes went around my curves. He licked his full lips. I paused not wanting to tell him. My mother, before she passed away, named me *America*. It sounded patriotic, but I dreaded the first day of school when the teachers would do roll call. They would reach America and I saw the perplexed look on their faces. It was as if they weren't reading it right.

"America…?" Teachers used to ask incredulously.

All the kids would laugh. The first week of school, my name would be the butt of everyone's joke. That was the only thing they could joke about with me because I was cute, and popular with the boys and some of the girls liked me.

"My name's America, okay?"

I was waiting for him to laugh. Surprisingly, he didn't.

"I like that, America… God bless America," he said.

I smiled.

Omar stayed awhile when we got to my crib, and I took the groceries to my aunt. We talked for hours that day and many more. Soon, we became inseparable. He became my heart. We spent days together, talking, laughing, and falling in love with each other.

My thoughts were with him everyday of his incarceration. I visited him often trying to keep his mind at ease and reminded him what he had waiting for him when he got out. I couldn't wait to nestle in his arms again. Part of me was missing every day without him. I yearned for his touch, and to feel his breath against mines. I hungered for our bodies to be entwined, and for him to devour me. My pussy throbbed uncontrollably, and my panties were saturated with escaping juices thinking of him.

I was trying to cool off in the shower, but it got no better. I was so fucking horny there was an ache in my body that refused to leave. It got intense because in less than twenty-four hours my baby will be loving every curve, shape and inch of me until my pussy put him to sleep.

Four years of waiting, and being faithful to my boo. I sighed ready to explode. This scene had repeated so many times, I lost count of how many times I masturbated alone in the dark with the toys I had purchased over the years. Visions of Omar grinding and gyrating between my legs kept rewinding in my mind. Many nights I had stayed up sleepless, thinking of Omar, a pillow between my thighs while fondling my tits.

There were many nights of long cold showers. Being horny and alone without my man around was a most unbearable situation. I'd pour my pain into songs and poems, many days and evenings. The words were so emotional, repeating them filled me with sadness and became unbearable.

I smiled removing the showerhead and putting one leg up on the porcelain tub. Then I positioned the spurting water next to my animated kitty-cat, setting the speed just right as the water rushed against my pulsating pussy. Moans escaped my lips and I moved my free hand in between my thighs, masturbating my clit. Moving my fingertips faster in a circular motion, I was losing control. The spurting water against my over-excited pussy lips did the trick.

"Ah, hmm... Hmm. Ooh yeah! Oh God, I missed you so much, dear Omar," I cried, having an explosive orgasm.

Thoughts of my man making love to me were embedded in my mind. His dick prints were etched on my vagina walls and made me feel like he was inside. But tonight there'd be no further need for pretension. My man finally will be home after four long years of keeping his pussy pure and tight. I peed while my lips purred.

Omar

Pussy was the only thing on my mind. True story. Four years of not getting any, and I was thirsty for my boo-boo. My sexual desires got even stronger within the week of my release. I thought about my girl everyday, all day. She was the first and last thing on my mind when I woke up and went to sleep at nights. She was the only reason why I survived in here for the last four years.

America came to see my like twice a month, and I loved her for that. The trip upstate was about seven hours to Franklin Correctional facility in Malone, New York. Sometimes she did the drive alone, or took the greyhound to come see me. America always came to see me looking her finest. I really hated to see her leave.

Her visiting me was a gift and a curse. Seeing my woman looking so fine and sexy was a true gift. I couldn't do nothing but give her a hug, a kiss, and hold hands across the table. My dick was so hard, it felt like it wanted to escape from my pants and rip into her warm flesh. But there was no excessive display of affection during visits, my curse for being here.

Pictures of America, her songs, and letters plastered my cell wall. Guards and cellmates envied me because I got at least three letters every week. Sometimes a poem or a song came from America. Every night before lights out, I read the soothing words she had written, fantasizing about warm days and long nights with her.

I would stare at a picture of the two of us together taken at Coney Island in the spring of '98, against the background of a painting of Jay Z holding up cash. We were young and looked cozy like we had no care. I was hugged up on her and both our smiles were ear to ear. The picture cost me five bucks but being locked up, it proved to be worth even more. It was the best of the good times. I was eighteen back then.

I remembered her attitude being a little rude when we first met. I thought she was cute. She was wearing lose fitted gray sweats, white T's and her feet looked small in a pair of white and blue Adidas. Her hair was in two long pigtails. The scent she had on made my heart do sprints. I saw her coming out of the store and couldn't let her just walk by me and not attempt to kick it to a girl so beautiful. America was trying to be reluctant, trying to spit fire as if she wasn't interested.

Up in my bunk, I continued peering at her photos. My abdominal muscle tightened as I reminisced over the first time we had sex. She was a virgin. I had been with lots of girls, but was intimate from the start. When it came to America, like she said, I made love to her. Before that I was just fucking girls.

America was different. My uncle, Ray gave me the keys to his basement apartment. Uncle Ray was a hustler like me and was always telling me how America was too fine a woman to ever let go.

"Boy, you treat her like the wonderful woman she is, and she'll treat you like the king you are. Always respect each other."

Uncle Ray was seventeen years my senior and he knew a lot about life. He was in and out of jail since I was in diapers. He had mad respect on the streets.

I brought America to my uncle's crib on a Friday night. She was the most nervous fifteen-year old I'd ever seen. We had been together for six weeks, and this sexual yearning I had for her was suffocating me.

She was wearing a denim skirt and pink halter. Her hair was in two long pigtails. My uncle's comfortable, one-bedroom bachelor's pad, with big screen television, and a great stereo system, made a good impression. She became less tense once she realized we would be alone. Besides a leather couch, and his bedroom set, he had no furniture since he was hardly home.

Uncle Ray had a king size bed in the bedroom. A mirror and drawers stood above a burgundy area rug with gold trim was spread out on the parquet floor. My uncle wasn't much of a decorator, but his place was nice enough to make America fill comfortable in.

I led America to the bedroom. She quietly followed. Then she touched me, stared at me with her soft brown eyes and smiled. She knew what time it was. I had made it all clear. I never wanted to mislead her in anything.

"Are you nervous?"

"A little," she giggled.

Her soft touch had me hard. I caressed her gently when we were near the bed. She felt relaxed in my arms. But I wanted to make sure she was ready for what was about to happen.

"Are you sure you're ready, America?"

Her eyes took on an aura of innocence, telling me that I'd have to lead and she'd follow me into our first sexual episode. I wouldn't have it any other way. It was a honor to be her first, but what I hoped for was to be her last. She smiled faintly and nodded.

America sat next to me on the bed. I moved slowly, but lust wanted me to tear off her clothes, skip foreplay and fuck the shit out of her. Slow down my beating heart, she was different and I had to take my time.

I moved my hand up and down her smooth open thigh. My dick pulsated in my pants. I pressed my lips against hers and kissed her good. Our tongues tangled, wrestling as our breathing became one. I moved my hand further up her skirt until I felt the wetness of her panties. She flinched but didn't pull away.

She stared at me for a moment. I was wondering what was on her mind. She remained silent and I prayed that she wanted to continue. My dick was harder than the man of steel and if I couldn't get pussy, then I'd be in for a very bad night. Fortunately, she wanted to continue. America positioned herself on her back and braved a smile.

"I want you to be my first, Omar. I love you and I trust you," she softly whispered.

I pulled up her skirt, and removed her panties unhurriedly. She reclined with her head amongst the plush pillows on the bed. Her breath became louder her round breast smiled at me while her curly pussy hairs, barely covered moistened lips. They seemed clamped together tightly like a bank vault after closing. I definitely knew she was pure now.

I moved my lips closer to her honey brown skin, kissing her gently starting with her belly button. She moaned a little. My hands slid up her chest, she cupped her hands over mine, and pressed them to her breasts. Her tits tasted like soft fruits.

Spreading her legs wider, I began kissing her inner thighs. Her breathing turned into moaning when my tongue and lips neared her pussy.

I don't normally be eating out pussy, but I was willing to go all the way with her. She trusted me and was giving me something she couldn't take back.

I gradually opened up the lips between her young thighs with my tongue and mouth. With my head nestled between her warm thighs my tongue began piercing into her, and she released enough juices for me to drink.

"Ooh… Ah… Ooh yes this feels real good oh… Oh yes!"

America gripped my head and held it in place. With her thighs clamped around my ears, she dug her nails into my shoulders and screamed, "Jesus Christ…Oh God yes!"

I looked up and smiled when I saw her beautiful eyes rolled back in her head. I smiled when all I saw was pure ivory. My dick never felt so hard I thought it was about to rip through my boxers. America looked like she was still in la-la land after my licking. I stood up dropped my jeans, soon afterwards my boxers fell. I stared at America in all her glory and held my big black dick.

America's eyes were wide when she saw my erection ready for action. She was beautiful, and untouched. And my dick was extra fucking hard with just that thought alone.

"You got condoms right?"

"Yeah."

I went into my pants pocket on the floor and removed a box of Magnums. I hastily tore the box open, removing a condom and ripped it open. Then I rolled the condom back on my thickness, and climbed atop positioning myself between her inviting thighs. She was tight I tried to slide right into her, but it wasn't happening. America gasped and grabbed my shoulders. I held my weight off of her, and continued to ease inches of myself into her. It was pleasurable but it was work.

"Ouch ugh… Oh shit! Omar slower… Oh baby, baby please, it's too big!"

Her eyes were tightly shut while her nails dug into my shoulders. I pushed a few more inches into her, slowly opening her bit by bit. I could feel her juices all over me. It took an hour of slow pushing before finally getting into my rhythm. A few more minutes and her hot, tight love-box caused an immense explosion like I never felt before. We didn't have sex for another two months after the first time. America proved to be worth the wait.

Lying in my bunk staring at her photo thinking about the first time we had sex got me hard. My hand was in my pants holding my thick, pulsating dick. I was slowly jerking-off and staring at America's picture.

"You 'bout to see home soon, and be in some pussy again, and you in here beatin' off. Go head wit' that, Soul," my cellmate, Rahmel interjected.

"Yo, this shit feel like a fucking dream, son. I can't believe a nigga's 'bout to go home," I said.

"Soul, you gettin' your freedom again, and your woman stayed by your side and held you down for four years. You're a blessed man. What's the first thing you gonna do when you get out?"

"Shit, I'm gonna take my woman and fuck her till my dick can't work anymore. And then I'm gonna wake up and do it all over again. I gotta make up for long lost time."

Rahmel laughed.

"You think I'm joking. I'm backed up. Shit, I'm 'bout to put in some work."

Rahmel took a seat on the bottom of my cot. He hunched over with his elbows pressed against his knees, fingers clasped together, and looked at me with some importance deep in his gaze.

"You got a second chance at life. Soul, I envy you, man. I got another five years behind these walls. Been denied parole three times because of violence in my past. The system doesn't think I'm ready to be released early, ain't that some shit... white man judging my rehabilitation, like he God and shit. Being in here, they take everything from you. Shit, Soul, I miss the touch, the smell, the feel, and even the taste of a woman. My wife died when I was five years in this hellhole, they wouldn't even let me attend her damn funeral. They said I was a threat to society. Now my daughter's gone, her grandmother had some nerve, moving my little girl to Texas. How she gonna take the only thing a man has left, and move her a thousand miles away. I know I've told you this before, but I feel you need to hear it again, Soul."

"I guess I can take you one more night, Rah."

"In here you got nothing, but out there, you got everything to look forward to. I spent fifteen years trying to be a father to my daughter behind these walls… Impossible. I missed my daughter's first steps, her first words, and her first day of school, cause I'm contained miles away from her like some fuckin' animal allowing for our children to make the same mistake we made."

"I hear you Rah."

"Do right by America, Soul. And don't come back to this place. You got many talents, take advantage of them. And you're fortunate to have a love one waiting for you behind these walls. Don't make her do time with you ever again. She doesn't deserve it. Every strong black woman deserves her man by her side, not on the inside. It'll be hard Soul, but don't be discouraged. You're gonna have some challenges come your way… Challenges make life interesting. Overcoming them makes life meaningful. Take that with you when you leave this place and please stop jerking off now."

I nodded. Rahmel got so deep that when he talked to you, you just shut up and listen. An O.G from South Jamaica, Rahmel was in his mid thirties, and well respected wherever he went. He used to kick knowledge to his little brother, Omega and me, history, current events, politics, and science. I mean shit that you thought he didn't know anything about he would lecture it to us once in a while. But when beef came around, you saw a different side of him then. It was the side of him that got him locked up.

Back in the fall of 1990 Rahmel caught two bodies on Guy R. Brewer and South Road. One was a cop. I was ten when he was sentenced. In the beginning, Omega took it hard we both looked up to Rahmel. He used to call me his little brother and always treated me like family.

"Soul spit a lil' sump'n for me, since this being your last night in here," he said.

"No doubt, what you wanna hear?"

"Sump'n to keep me up," he smiled.

"Yo, yo, yo, as I sit alone and try to keep my head above the sky, insecurity got my mind blackened like a soulless child. I do my best to keep my head above the rest, when I feel too stressed, I break down and cry like the rest. Sometimes I feel my life is lost, everything I achieve comes wit' a cost. Wanna ball my fist and come storming out with full force, show the world that I'm much more than a ghetto ugly child. Got a few friends that I trust, while the rest I give dap to and keep tabs on the most. Determination in these eyes you see, bleed, seek richness and greatness with every breath that I breathe. My life was ignorant in my past, sex, drugs, and uneducated, I see why the white man laugh. My heart dies every time I get disrespected by my own kind, wish it was peace back on the block, when these fools' attitude is misery and just don't give a fuck, make this buck and shoot everything up! I wish the Lord's hands could come down and wash me from all my sins, but I feel the power of the devil sometimes possessing me within. Telling me it feels good son, damn, kill them niggas and hit them tight skins again. It's outrageous how some of us became so weak within!"

"Yeah, preach young blood, preach on. Follow your heart, believe in yourself and Him and the Lord will lead you from there," Rahmel said giving me dap. "Look out for my brother, Omega once you get home."

"True indeed, Rah. I'll make good on my word."